I0745988

J. A. JACKSON

The Grand Hotel
The Series Begins Lovers, Players…

First published by Ingram Sparks 2019

Copyright © 2019 by J. A. Jackson

All rights reserved. No part of this publication may be reproduced, stored or transmitted in any form or by any means, electronic, mechanical, photocopying, recording, scanning, or otherwise without written permission from the publisher. It is illegal to copy this book, post it to a website, or distribute it by any other means without permission.

This novel is entirely a work of fiction. The names, characters and incidents portrayed in it are the work of the author's imagination. Any resemblance to actual persons, living or dead, events or localities is entirely coincidental.

J. A. Jackson asserts the moral right to be identified as the author of this work.

J. A. Jackson has no responsibility for the persistence or accuracy of URLs for external or third-party Internet Websites referred to in this publication and does not guarantee that any content on such Websites is, or will remain, accurate or appropriate.

Designations used by companies to distinguish their products are often claimed as trademarks. All brand names and product names used in this book and on its cover are trade names, service marks, trademarks and registered trademarks of their respective owners. The publishers and the book are not associated with any product or vendor mentioned in this book. None of the companies referenced within the book have endorsed the book.

First edition

ISBN: ISBN: 978-1-946010-30-8

Editing by Rossi V. Jackson

This book was professionally typeset on Reedsy.
Find out more at reedsy.com

IngramSpark

Lightning Source™

an **INGRAM** Content company
More at lightningsource.com

*For Rossi V. Jackson Jr., who was with me when I wrote my first seven
novels. He was my editor, my best friend and my husband.
In loving memory of Rossi V. Jackson Jr. 1942 - 2015 ...*

"A friend loves at all times."
~ Proverbs 17:17

Contents

Acknowledgement

To my best friends' forever Jocelyn, Mary and Lenise. And to my big brother Randy, who is always my June bug. You "all" shine down on me always from heaven. I thank you and I miss you like crazy.

Next up I'd like to give out a big endless gratitude of thanks and appreciation for the wonderful support and editorial guidance of my editor the very knowledgeable Mr. Rossi V. Jackson.

I'd also like to say a special thanks to the incredible man in my life, my husband who believed in my writing and supported my dreams.

Also, to my mother and my father you blew the wind beneath my feet and made me enjoy learning, writing and living this life. God gave me you and you gave me unconditional love and support – Thank you.

Also, a special thanks to my sisters Kay, Shelia and Marie. I am so grateful to you for your support and love. And to my brothers Ray and Eric I thank you also.
   For Rossi, Randy, and Daddy & Mommy always….

To my readers and fans, I am forever grateful. Thank you.

The Grand Isles Ball – 1987...

Pearl La Cour strolled across the marbled lobby. She headed for the back entrance behind the elevators. It was rarely used, quiet and dimly lit. She hoped no one saw her. The window doors afforded a view to the overflow parking garage across the street. She furrowed her eyebrows, focusing attentively. There it was, the classic black Cadillac pulling in. She smiled at the memories of it.

Nervously she glanced at herself in the mirror across from her. She pushed back on her hair, making sure nothing was out of place.

She looked out of the door. The man crossed the street heading towards her.Pearl wanted to pinch herself. It was him.

His classic tuxedo clung to him in all the right places as he strolled gracefully towards her. She'd been waiting for him.

The man glanced through the door at her. Instant recognition dawned.

She was determined to speak to him alone. She glanced sideways. Her hand shook as she took a few steps toward the door.

A tall man, dressed impeccably with a commanding presence, walked up and opened the door.

The man she was waiting for greeted the other man.

Pearl watched as the two men engaged in conversation. She heard the tall man ask the man a barrage of questions.

Pearl closed her eyes, realizing that the man asking the questions wasn't in a hurry. She didn't want to seem impatient. When she opened her eyes the man she was waiting for was staring at her. He gave her a soft smile.

Pearl felt spellbound. She tilted her head and smiled back.

All at once an excited voice sliced the air.

"Mom!"

Pearl jumped.

A young girl's voice called out. "Mom, Dad said to come and look for you."

The man walked closer, stopped and he held Pearl's gaze.

"Ah! Lacey baby," she nervously exclaimed, glancing between her daughter and the man quickly.

The man raised his eyebrows, glanced at the little girl and then winked.

Pearl's eyes followed the man's line of sight. She flinched.

Her daughter Lacey was too excited about the message she carried to notice the man.

Silently the man smiled and nodded softly. He walked on.

"Mommy! Did you hear me? Dad is looking for you," Lacey said.

Pearl breathed out a sigh of relief. Her daughter Lacey hadn't even noticed who the man was. As usual, her daughter's mind was only on the mission her father had sent her out to accomplish. Making sure he kept track of where she was at all times.

Quickly Pearl hide her emotions behind her pretend smile. She was well aware of her hidden self. Her true self. Pearl knew the expression on her face was just a masquerade she hid behind pretending to be something that she was not, *happy*. She smiled with her thoughts thinking she made the world believe she was happy.

"Lacey Kadira Catherine La Cour I heard you," Pearl sternly said, clasping her daughter's hand in hers.

She turned and inspected her daughter. Gently, her fingers straightened and out of place strand of her hair.

"What does your father want, this time, Lacey honey?"

"Dad said he needs you to come and help him sort things out. He said to tell you he's lost without you. Edwina Johnson's mother is putting up a big stink because Dad said she can't judge the queen pageant this year. Dad said it's because her niece, Mona Johnson is competing. He doesn't want a big mess on his hands like last year, when Layla Cushman was a judge and her niece Leah Cushman won."

"No, I guess we don't," Pearl said with a smile, thinking about her husband Louis La Cour.

Suddenly Lacey twisted her hands and gave her mother the strangest look. "Mommy? What about the ghosts?"

"Ghosts? What is that Lacey?"

"Edwina Johnson said there's a lady that walks the halls of this hotel at night. And Maëlle said it was true."

Pearl stopped and took a step back. She kept watching her daughter.

"Maëlle said she's an angel who protects people. Do ghosts protect people Mommy? I thought angels were the protectors."

Pearl looked back at her daughter. She didn't want to show anxiety at the subject of her daughter's conversation. Maëlle Mallard was her daughter's best friend. The two had been friends from as far back as she could remember. The safest thing to do was to see where this was going. "What else did Maëlle say?"

"Well Maëlle said that an angel can be a ghost sometimes. If the situation calls for them to be one or if they need to protect someone."

"Well Lacey, I guess it sounds like Maëlle has really thought this one out," Pearl nodded. "Well, we'd better get back and help your father," she said leading the way.

Chapter 1

The Grand Isles Ball...December 1987
Players, Mischief Makers & other underachievers...

Pearl La Cour almost felt sorry for her husband Louis as she watched him from across the room. He looked lonely, sad and tormented, standing between the women expressing their discontent over some important issues.

Suddenly Louis La Cour looked her way. His eyes pleaded for help. Then, instantly, his gaze shifted, and his eyes alerted her.

She looked up just in time to see Monty Wildfire pushing his way through the crowd. She watched the crowd and she saw familiar faces from the tight-knit old families. Many had moved to California from the state of Louisiana.

"Pearl Fanay Andries, I thought that was you. I spotted you from across the room. My goodness, you look gorgeous in that dress," Monty said, grabbing her hand and making a show of kissing it. His eyes slowly roamed up and down her body.

Pearl wore a silver strapless, taffeta, floor length evening gown with a matching chiffon extra-long scarf that cascaded and flowed over her as she walked.

"Hi Monty, that's Mrs. Pearl Fanay Andries-La Cour" she said. "I'm married remember?”

Monty's dark eyes observed her. He rubbed his jaw as he licked his lips. Damn Pearl, I'm trying to forget! He thought taking a deep breath.

Monty Wildfire was a very handsome man, rich, educated and well mannered.

“You know Monty; I will never understand why you never use my married name.”

Monty laughed out. He liked to laugh. “And I will never understand why Louis always leaves you alone at events like this. Doesn't he know how yummy you are?”

Pearl rolled her eyes.

Someone cleared their throat.

A tall man in a tuxedo walked past them.

Pearl's heart pounded like a hammer in her chest. The man she was waiting for earlier walked past. He was in deep conversation with Mrs. Tobias Johnson. She was a blue rinsed haired elderly matron who always insisted on everyone calling her Mrs. Tobias Johnson.

The man held Mrs. Tobias Johnson's arm with his arm while helping her walk back to her table.

Pearl knew she stared at them a little too long. She shrugged and turned back to Monty. Out of the corner of her eyes, she caught sight of a woman in a hot pink dress with an intense stare at the back of Monty's head, coming toward them.

“Oh Monty, don't look now, but I think the president of your fan club is coming.”

The woman in the hot pink dress headed their way as if she was being hotly pursued by an army of giants. She stopped abruptly and quickly extended her hand. “Hi, I'm Celica Baptiste. I'm Monty Wildfire's date for tonight.”

Monty coughed. “Just for tonight,” he mumbled under his breath.

It was obvious that Monty Wildfire was trying to pretend he wasn't with the woman. Her loud hot pink dress stood out badly at the

Christmas Ball.

Pearl didn't bat an eye. She knew what it was like not to be fashion conscious. She hadn't been born into money. She'd married it. "Hello Celica. I'm Pearl, Mrs. Pearl La Cour."

Celica Baptiste's body build was awkward. She had manly shoulders that seemed too large for her body. The cut of her dress didn't fit her body. But her smile was pretty. It lit up her face.

"You know Celica; I believe I've heard your name before. You are on the board at the Valley Women's Guild?"

Celica smiled brightly and nodded. "Yes, I still am," she announced with pride.

Pearl smiled. "I think the Guild does a great job helping the community. Your meetings are always charged with raw energy."

"You're telling me. Sometimes I think I should bring my boxing gloves," she said, her eyes growing wide. "I've seen you at a couple of meetings also and I've always wanted to talk to you. But I always have to help the Secretary. She's my mother's sister. Aunt Dolly Baptiste. She practically raised me."

Monty Wildfire cleared his throat. "Too much information Celica my dear," he warned.

Pearl coughed under her breath.

Monty ignored Pearl's smirk. "Pearl darling," he said. We'd like to arrange a private meeting with you and Louis. We have a proposal for a charity fundraising event. Tell you what, I'll call Louis and arrange a date."

Pearl's thoughts raced. She hoped it wasn't another stupid suggestion to hold a charity auction. At the last charity auction Monty used the event to unload a shipment of bubble gum machines that he couldn't sell. "Okay, sure Monty," she turned and nodded at Celica. "It was nice to meet you."

Monty hesitated. His voice was sympathetic. "Celica do me a big favor and go check our seats. Make sure there is a reserve sign on them. This place is filling up fast. Oh, and grab us both a glass of champagne."

"Sure, Monty."

Monty waited and a second after Celica was out of his sight, he leaned over close and whispered. "Pearl, I saw how you looked at that man that just walked by."

Pearl stiffened for only a moment. "I don't know what you're talking about Monty," she said taking a step back.

"You lie well," Monty said, observing her. His teeth sparkled like the just cleaned brilliance of white-walled tires. "I know Louis keeps you locked up in that big house with his mother and those kids watching you all day," his words flowed off of his tongue. "You know; I do understand all about the ignored housewife. You need some fun. I'm the man for your fun and games Pearl."

Pearl stared at him dumbfounded. She'd given Monty way more attention than he should have been given that evening.

"You and your date have a nice evening Monty!" she hissed out under her breath. Her eyes flashed in rage as she quickly turned indignantly to put some distance between them.

Chapter 2

Running Amok and Asking for a Favor...

Pearl's encounter with Monty Wildfire had left her in a really bad mood. She straightened her back, determined to lift her spirits. She wandered out of the ballroom into the hallway. The ladies' room was just down the corridor on the left, she remembered.

With a deep sigh, she noticed a liquor bar set up just outside of the ballroom door. She wasn't a big drinker. But after her ordeal with Monty, she needed something refreshing.

"Sir would you please pour some ginger ale into a wine glass for me?" she asked, glancing at herself in the gold mirror behind the bar. Her eyes zoomed in on her lipstick. She needed to fix it. Out of the corner of her eye, she saw movement. She focused intensely and noticed her son Nicholas La Cour.

Pearl turned around. Nicholas was down the corridor in a corner rough housing with another boy.

Nicholas' best friend Quinn Rolandis stood trying to block the view. Pearl was sure Quinn had put Nichols up to it.

Determined, Pearl quickly made her way to several people.

Pearl heard the boy's voice as she fast approached.

"Stop it, stop it! Nicholas! Leave me alone," the boy yelled wailing his arms.

They say that someone who is afraid can sometimes harness great strength. The boy did.

Wham Bam!

In a flash, the boy's hand balled into a fist and it made contact with the side of Nicholas' face, not once but twice.

"You hit me you stupid jerk!" Nicholas whined, grabbing the boy by the collar.

"Nicholas let him go. Your mother is coming!" Quinn hissed out hastily.

He turned around quickly. "Hello, Mrs. La Cour. What a lovely dress you're wearing. If you don't mind my saying so, I believe you purchased it at Macys. I know because my grandmother was looking at the same one. But they didn't carry her size," Quinn said trying to make polite conversation.

"Quinn, I'm sure you are not interested in my dress," she said sternly turning her attention to her son.

Pearl closed the distance between her and Nicholas. "Nicholas, let that boy go now!"

"Mrs. La Cour, Nicholas was trying to make me eat that plant. He's mad because Snooky Toussaint asked me to escort her down the coronation aisle when it's her turn to march."

"I am not mad that Snooky choose Newt Mallard," Nicholas snapped. His voice choked. "I'm mad because …" Tears flashed in his eyes.

Pearl looked taken back. Her heart went out to her son. He was hurt that Snooky had chosen Newt over him. But still, she knew Quinn's influence when she saw it. Nicholas had been beating Newt up at the urging of Quinn. She was sure of it. Her voice was stern. "Nicholas, you need to apologize to Newt now."

"I don't need to apologize to Newt Mallard. Not after what he just did to me.

"Nicholas, you forget who you're talking too? I didn't ask. I'm telling you, you will apologize to Newt now," Pearl commanded. She hesitated. "You know your sister is best friends with Newt's cousin Maëlle Mallard?" She asked but didn't wait for a response. "I'm sure Maëlle won't be happy to hear about your bullying her cousin."

"But Mom, you don't know what Newt said," Nicholas said in his defense.

A man whistled behind them. "Your mother wants you to apologize son and I think you should do it. A gentleman should always take the high road. Don't you think so son?"

Nicholas' eyes darted toward the familiar voice. "Well, yes sir. All right then," he shrugged.

Nicholas took a step back, adjusted his coat jacket and cleared his throat. "Newt, I apologize," he said with deep remorse. "I didn't mean to try to make you eat dirt just because Snooky Toussaint likes you enough to ask you to be her escort for the coronation march. Even if I still can't see what she sees in you," he hesitated and quickly added. "I'm truly sorry."

Newt grinned and smoothed his jacket. "Thanks, Nicholas, your apology is accepted."

Louis Antoine Nicolas Avoyelles La Cour was a tall man, over six feet tall. He was well dressed in a formal tux for the night's event. His wavy black hair was neatly trimmed.

He stood beside his wife Pearl and wanted to pinch himself each time he realized how lucky he was to have Pearl. She was the love of his life. He took his wife's hand and kissed it.

Then he cleared his throat. "You boys had better hurry. The coronation march will begin soon."

Newt shrugged. "I'd better go find Snooky. I bet she's been looking for me," he said strolling away with a confident stance.

Louis squeezed closer to his wife Pearl, his arm protectively encircling her waist. He went to give her a kiss and noticed his son. "Nicholas, don't you think you and Quinn should get going?"

"Nay Dad, we don't have any place to go," Nicholas said. Remember, Quinn and I don't have escorts.

Louis chuckled softly. "Well now Nicholas your old dad kind of needs a big favor," he winked. "I just left a Miss Lucy Mondragon and her cousin Miss Jade Mondragon waiting for two very handsome young men to come and escort them in the coronation march," he hesitated. "And I sort of promised them that you and Quinn were available."

"Dad are you serious?" Nicholas exclaimed.

"Yes, I am," Louis smiled softly. "So are my favorite two guys up for doing me a big favor. What do you say? Help the old man out of a jam?"

"Yes!" Nicholas and Quinn exclaimed simultaneously.

"Well, what are you waiting for guys? Get going." Louis commanded. Pearl and Louis watched the boys run off.

Louis turned to Pearl. "I know you probably think I let Nicholas off the hook. But I overheard Newt teasing Nicholas and Quinn earlier about not getting asked by any of the girls to be their escort," he said. "I'm sorry if you're angry at me my dear."

Pearl leaned over and kissed Louis softly on the lips. "Oh Louis, no, I couldn't be mad at you. The boys looked so happy when you told them they had escorts. And it will keep both of them busy tonight. At least until Mother Kahina Laveau takes all the children to the slumber party."

The children's annual slumber party was as famous as the annual Grand Isles Gala. The children looked forward to spending the night away from home and parents. And parents looked forward to the night of privacy the event afforded them.

Louis bent his head in close and kissed her again. His hand on her lower back pulled her closer. "I take my husband duties, pleasing my wife, seriously."

Monty Wildfire watched the couple from a distance and tried to cool his anger. Life wasn't fair. He wanted Pearl so bad he ached from the pain in his heart. How did men like Louis get women like Pearl?

Peeking from behind a thick heavy leafed fern, he clenched his jaw.

He couldn't help thinking how much better Pearl would have looked having his arms wrapped around her.

Monty's eyes glazed over with an expressionless dream like stare. -had no idea how attractive she was to him. Caught up in his thoughts, he licked his lips as he thought about what she would look like naked, draped across his bed. The corners of his lips curled up with his thoughts. His hands clenched into tight fists by his side. Someday I'll possess Pearl, mind body and soul, he thought.

In a moment's notice, a voice sliced the air. "Louis and Pearl, I believe you two have an admirer!" Detective Manny Rebrand greeted them as he pointed across where Monty stood.

"Oh, don't mind Monty. He thinks no one can see him hiding behind that fern," Louis chuckled as he shook Manny's hand. "Pearl and I had been wondering when one of San Jose's finest would show up tonight. It's good to see you again."

"Yes, it is good to see you, Manny," Pearl said as she warmly gave Detective Manny a hug.

"I'm always glad to attend the Grand Isle Ball and watch over things as your official detective," Detective Manny said assuredly.

Monty rushed over. "Ahhhh MMM, Detective Manny," he said, clearing his throat. "I was just enjoying how good Louis and Pearl danced together. You can tell they've had lessons."

"Yeah, I'm sure you were Monty," Detective Manny said, "You know Monty there is a law against being a peeping tom."

Pearl stifled a giggled.

Detective Manny gave Monty a hard stare and said. "Monty, I can't watch you all night, so you just stay out of trouble, Okay?"

Monty slowly nodded agreement.

Detective Manny turned and caught Louis' eye. He put his hand on his shoulder. "Louis, I'll leave you now. I have to go and check out things and make my rounds. After that maybe I'll get a couple of dances in before I leave. You haven't seen Clare Palling, have you?"

"Yes, she's in the office we set up behind the stage," Louis said. "I guess you're planning on asking her to dance?"

Detective Manny grinned wide. "Yep, I sure will. Well, I guess I'll be going."

Pearl and Louis turned and watched as Detective Manny walked away.

"He's sweet on Clare, isn't he?" Pearl asked.

Louis nodded. "And I don't think Ulysses will be happy about that."

The couple stared at each other and laughed.

Monty sidled in closer with a smug expression. "How very lovely to catch husband and wife together. Louis, did Pearl tell you I wanted to set up a meeting with the two of you?" His eyes sought out Pearl's and held them.

"No Monty," Louis shrugged. His body language conveyed that he wasn't interested in carrying on a conversation.

"Sorry, no I haven't Monty," Pearl glanced up apologetically. "I haven't had a chance to tell him."

Monty's mouth thinned. "Well, Pearl darling, I won't hold that against you."

In reality, Pearl could do no wrong in Monty's eyes. He masked his emotions as he watched the two of them. Pearl was the perfect woman. Soft-spoken, biddable and accommodating, just like now. Monty knew Pearl was only kissing Louis back out of duty. Pearl was everything Monty ever wanted in a woman. She'd make him the perfect wife. If she was his he would mold her into what was ultimately a prefect wife.

He cleared his throat. "You know Louis, the idea I have will make us both a lot of money. We should talk about it now."

Louis was blunt. "No Monty not now. Can't you see I'm a man who is spending time with his wife?"

Monty laughed softly as if to reassure himself. He realized Louis was ignoring him. He glanced at Pearl and quickly thought of something to engage her in the conversation.

He cleared his throat. "Pearl, I'm sure you can see the importance of our meeting right now, especially since the venture would involve using a charity close to your heart."

Pearl turned and glanced at him. Her eyes gleamed. She blinked several times.

Monty knew he had her interest. "Yes, I can see Pearl at the helm of things running her charity and taking care of the needs of the community."

"Monty!" Louis said brusquely. "Stop interfering in my wife's concentration. Can't you see she's busy kissing me right now?" he asked but didn't wait for a response. "Go away!" he commanded.

He realized his tone might have been harsh. He stopped kissing Pearl turned and leveled his gaze on Monty. He lowered his voice. "Monty tonight is the Grand Isles Christmas Gala, and I would like to have another dance with my beautiful wife."

"Yes, your wife is beautiful," Monty thought. He looked around making sure no one saw the way he looked at Pearl.

Monty cleared his throat loudly.

"Will you excuse us, Monty?" Louis asked.

Not waiting for a response, as he grasped his wife in his arms and kissed her for Monty's benefit. "You know Pearl, when I look at you, I see my happiness."

Pearl felt herself sway when Louis' arms released her. "Louis…I," she whispered, her lips dry, her mouth parched.

In a second Monty's eyes flashed with a dark coldness. He breathed out defensively. "Oh, by the way Louis, I was told to tell you to start the ceremony to select the queen now. You don't have time to dance with Pearl. But don't worry I'll dance with your wife."

Challenging Monty stood in front of Louis.

Louis laughed mockingly. "Oh, really Monty?"

Just then Louis reached out and grabbed Pearl's arm, pulling her close. He stared back at Monty, his voice challenging. "I'm off to dance with my wife. Unless of course, you are telling me not to Monty?"

Monty shrugged and quickly stepped aside.

"Bye Monty," Pearl said brushing past him.

Monty watched Pearl eagerly pull Louis' arm around her waist. His fist clenched tight. He lowered his hand behind his back so that no one would see, as he watched Louis walk away with Pearl

Chapter 3

Old Friends the Mondragon Family & the Baptiste family...

Two huge gold fleurs-de-lis hung on each of the fluted concrete columns that stood on either side of the massive double doors of the Grand ballroom.

Tonight, the Grand ballroom will host the Annual Grand Isles Christmas Gala. The Junior Royal Court children's pageant will be held first, this event will be followed by the Grand Finale' of the festivities, The Royal Queen Pageant.

Across the massive foyer, around the curved formal grand staircase, hang a stunning massive rock crystal chandelier. It heralded a welcoming entry to the smaller twenty-five thousand square foot Regency ballroom it held at the top.

The Regency Ballroom had been set up with a dance floor that opened into a magnificent enclosed outdoor garden. The outdoor garden was set-up for the adults only.

The massive foyer heading to the two main ballrooms held many seating areas. Crisp white tablecloth lined tables set up in cabaret style with cozy high-back leather chairs were as far as the eye could see. Opulent columns for privacy were arranged throughout the seating area.

At the bottom of the grand stairwell, a man and woman chatted.

Milady Egan had been born beautiful. Her skin and hair were flawless. Her soft gray eyes smiled brightly at the man standing next to her. She affectionately called him her sweetheart, because in her island home of Montserrat, once a proposed marriage union was recognized, the couple was referred to as being sweethearts. She smiled with her thoughts remembering when her grandmother Ada D'Abreu had told her that Thor Egan had asked to marry her.

Thor Egan had mesmerizing, deep green eyes. He stood over six feet three inches tall. His hand reached up and pushed back a stray strand of jet-black wavy hair. He'd meant to have his hair cut before he attended the ball tonight, but he was busy working on a project and he'd forgotten. The barber he trusted had been over-booked by too many clients. Most of who were in attendance that night.

He gazed disconcertingly back at his wife. "Kienan is too fascinated by all these military men in their formal uniforms for my liking. They could be filling his head with all kinds of military nonsense," his voice betrayed his agitation. "The boy's mind is young and impressionable. I don't want them filling his head with military ideas. I feel I should go over and remind him his mother has her doctorate degree and his father has his master's degree. We expect him to bring home the same or better, not join the military. Don't we wife."

Milady Egan's steel gray eyes smiled gracefully back at her husband. She knew her husband was very protective of their only son and he took his parenting very seriously. The only other man she'd ever known Thor to consider as good enough to be their son's mentor was Louis La Cour. "Thor, our son is just curious dear. Don't worry. He's a chip off of the old block. He knows he's going to college," Milady's island accent sounded like musical notes carried on the wind.

Milady drew in a breath and waved her hand. Out of the corner of her eyes, she saw two men entering. "Oh, look sweetheart. David Creek and Ulysses Portillo have just arrived. You wanted to talk to them."

Thor Egan looked in the direction of his wife's gaze. He smiled brightly. He respected the opinions of the two men who had just arrived. He felt their minds were as sharp as his own and therefore were worthy of his engaging in conversations with.

The two men approached.

"Thor Egan, you are just the man I wanted to talk with," Ulysses Portillo's robust voice sliced the air.

"It's good to see you, Ulysses," Thor greeted him.

Slowly David Creek strolled over. And immediately shook Thor's hand. He smiled politely as he leaned over. His voice was laden with prickled anticipation. "Sorry Thor, I've just been asked to dance by a very beautiful lady," he said with an excited thrill in his voice. "But don't worry; I'll catch up with the two of you shortly."

Milady touched her husband's arm and eyed him thoughtfully. She saw her chance to freshen up her lipstick. "Thor, I'll let you speak to Ulysses in private. I have wanted to go to the lady's room anyway," she said making her exit.

Milady marveled at the huge assembly of gathering guests. She nodded numerous greetings as she made her way across the vast foyer. Before she knew it, she was swallowed up in the gathering crowd.

XXX

The Grand Regency ballroom held a curtain wall separating the stage area where the main pageant event of the night would take place. Another part of the Regency Ballroom had been set aside for a dance floor and DJ area. It was abuzz with energy as the Annual Grand Isles Christmas Ball got under way. The DJ played Zydeco Boogaloo Zydeco and everyone in the place was dancing. Grandfathers, grandmothers, fathers, mothers, daughters and sons all danced their best moves on the dance floor.

XXX

A half hour later the fast-paced music came to an end.

Loud happy babble slowly faded into soft giggles and murmurs sounded out as the crowd slowly dispensed from the dance floor.

"Oh Lord, I'm glad that song ended. I almost killed myself dancing," Grand-mere Catherine said, making her way out of the ballroom. "Come along Lacey and Maëlle. Let's go out into the foyer and find a seat."

Lacey waived her hand. "Grand-mere, can we sit over there by the grand stairwell?"

"Great idea Lacey," Maëlle Mallard exclaimed. "We'll be right under the chandelier. We'll shine like star people."

Grand-mere Catherine smiled softly. She knew the chandelier's brilliance wasn't the only thing the two little girls were after. "Sure. I know you and Maëlle want to people watch."

The two girls headed for their chairs and quickly sat down.

Instantly a commotion ensued at the doorway bottom of the stairwell.

"Grand-mere look, Lacey pointed. "That girl looks like my Enchanted Evening Indri Creole Doll you gave me for my birthday."

Grand-mere Catherine's eyes followed in the direction where her granddaughter pointed. She caught sight of the Baptiste Family making their grand entrance.

The Baptiste family's only daughter Katrina Baptiste was the object of her granddaughter Lacey's fascination.

Katrina had just turned eighteen on that December 1, 1987. Her entry into the Annual Grand Isles Christmas Queen Pageant was well talked about in the close-knit community. Growing up, Katrina had been a shy girl. That all changed two years ago when her mother Pauline Baptiste entered her into a professional modeling school. Overnight, Katrina blossomed and became an assertive attention-seeking opportunist.

Grand-mere Catherine watched as Katrina put on her best floor show. She slowly gave her best catwalk, attention-getting strut, in her pink satin evening gown with a white faux fur bolero jacket. As she sparkled and lit up the room just like a Creole Barbie Doll should, she meandered between tables greeting friends. It was obvious Katrina knew she was the best-dressed pageant contestant of the night.

The Baptiste family was known for their large real estate holdings. But the real family fortune had been made in banking and insurance. Jean Baptiste family could trace their roots back to the Spanish land grants of 1855.

Her mother, Pauline Baptiste, followed closely behind Katrina smiling widely. Her expertly dyed blond hair looked natural. It complemented her beautiful tan skin. She wore expensive jewelry and held her head high as she closely followed behind her daughter.

Katrina's father Jean Baptiste brought up the rear end of their little family party. He sported a briskly trimmed mustache and deep wavy black hair parted on the side. His gray-green eyes sparkled. He was a tall man with a fluid grace that some men are just born with.

As if on cue he spotted Grand-mere Catherine. His eyes were candid as he stared back at her. He lifted a brow as his eyes narrowed into slits holding her attention. Quickly he closed the distance between them.

"Good evening Grand-mere Catherine. How are you? This seems to be an exceptional turnout," Jean Baptiste said as his gray-green eyes regarded her appraisingly. "Exceptional, exceptional," he repeated without waiting for her response.

"This is an exceptional turn-out this year Jean," Catherine said looking around the room.

"To be perfectly honest Catherine I was admiring how well you look tonight," he said with a glimmer of amusement in his eyes.

"Jean you are still the flirt," she softly laughed.

Jean flushed. "But this is a success. Louis is using every ballroom in the hotel. It looks like folks are crowded into both the main level and the upper levels. I'm sure I won't be able to spot Louis in this crowd."

"Yes, but don't forget, there is the outdoor garden just off of the

Regency Ballroom. It's Louis' favorite spot. It is set up in a grand opulence romantic theme just for those of us who are over the age of eighteen," she laughed.

"I heard Pauline mention that room. Is it very elegant and romantic?"

Catherine giggled. "Yes, I've seen it. The room feels charming and romantically spell binding with its soft outdoor lighting and elegant romantic music. It can make a married couple fall back in love again."

He thought for a moment. "I've heard that too, from my wife Pauline. I guess I had better make sure I have a dance with her there," he said, as he anxiously let his gaze look around.

Grand-mere Catherine noted the anxiousness in his voice. "Jean, if you're looking for my son Louis, I believe you should find him there in the garden room."

"Yes. Yes, thank you. But if he isn't there?" he asked shifting uneasily.

She nodded. "If he isn't there with Pearl then he's gone back to the office he has behind the stage in the Grand Ballroom. He and Mrs. Palling, the accountant, have an office there."

Relief showed on his face. His lips quivered into a smile. "Thanks Grand-mere Catherine," he paused. "Oh, by the way, I've always admired you, Catherine. We've been friends for a long time. Haven't we?"

She fought back a smile. She could read his thoughts as if they were her own. "I know when there is something troubling you Jean. What's on your mind?"

"Remington Breaux. He's back in town. I believe he will be coming here tonight," he said shaking his head. "I thought you should know."

Grand-mere Catherine's steel gray eyes stared back at him.

"Thanks, Jean. I owe you one."

"Don't worry about it, Catherine". He smiled softly and started to turn away.

"Jean," Catherine softly said. "I saw your baby sister Celica Baptiste earlier with that Monty Wildfire fellow."

Jean's lips tightened into a sneer. "That girl won't listen. I've warned her time and time again about Monty Wildfire," his eyes were angry. "He's nothing but a hustler and a user."

He felt her eyes on him. He looked up and his eyes softened. "But the man is a charmer, and until she realizes he's using her, there is not much I can do. You know how it is with family Catherine."

"Yes Jean, I know exactly what you're saying," she said nodding.

Jean hesitated as if to say more. He smiled softly and then turned and walked away.

XXX

A short distance away, Pauline Baptiste grabbed a glass of wine off of a passing tray. She was just going to lift the glass to her lips when her eyes caught sight of the young woman approaching her.

"Ming…Ming Mondragon. It is so good to see you again," Pauline Baptiste cried out pulling her warmly into an embrace. "How's my favorite Mondragon?"

"Oh Pauline, it's so good to see you too. I'm just fine," Ming smiled tenderly. Pauline Baptiste was like a second mother to her. "I see the Baptiste family is out tonight. And just look at Katrina. She looks so elegant. I know she'll win the Royal Queen competition tonight."

"Goodness, I hope so," Pauline shrugged. "I just wish she'd listened to me and let me change the color of her hair. A few honey amber highlights would have given her extra points with the male judges. I'm sure of it," she smiled. "Men love that sort of thing."

"Yes, but Pauline, not many women can wear honey blond hair like you. You are the only woman I know who can wear blond streaked hair and make it look classic and elegant with no black roots."

Pauline laughed. "Me? With black roots? I wouldn't allow the undertaker to bury me if I had black roots."

Both ladies laughed simultaneously.

Pauline threw her head back. Her laughter died as she stared back with a pure expression of shock registering on her face.

Ming's eyes looked in the direction of her gaze. She looked up intently as the buxom woman walked into the open foyer.

"Damn," Pauline's voice held a note of steel as she shot Ming a warning look. "Don't look now, but competition for our husband's affections has arrived.

Ming stared critically in the direction of Pauline's gaze. "Who is that?"

Pauline shook her head with a sigh. "You've heard of that bible story about that Delilah creature? You know the one who seduced Samson."

Ming nodded, but kept her eyes on Delilah as she breezed across the room.

Pauline gave her a sincere matronly stare. "Well consider Delilah Deauville as a real-life version of the bible's original Delilah," she paused. "Only be careful. This one not only seduces men; she also enjoys seducing women."

Ming's jaw tensed as she stared dumbfounded back at Pauline. Her eyes held complete wonder. A second later she tilted her head and stole another gaze at Delilah Deauville.

Pauline noticed Ming gazing. "Yes Ming, there are women that are into that sought of thing and Delilah Deauville is definitely one. Don't become too chummy with her. You have a tendency to be too trusting of people," she warned her.

The music picked up a beat, a modern guitar rhythm, morphing a throbbing melody that sent an electrifying energy into the air.

Pauline took Ming by the arm and led her over to other guests and quickly made introductions.

Ming and Pauline never saw the scene unraveling behind them.

Boldly, Delilah Deauville strode confidently around the huge foyer. She oozed a sensual aura that appealed to the male sex.

A man walked up to her. He was square-jawed handsome. He wore his wavy black hair pulled back in a ponytail. He had a commanding aggressive power about him. Raw sexual energy poured out of him.

All at once Delilah threw back her head laughing with the familiar man.

Delilah Deauville looked sexy, seductive, elegant and regal, in a red sequined evening dress with a chiffon scarf that draped like a sari around her. Her evening gown gracefully exposed her full bosom superbly.

It was evident in her assured manner that Delilah knew she was the envy of every woman present.

Finally, Delilah kissed the man on the cheek. She left him and floated over to greet someone else she knew.

All at once Delilah waived her arms in a grand sweeping gesture as she recognized her.

"Pauline Baptiste, is that you? It's wonderful to see you again," Delilah said as her hand reached out to clasp her in a hug. Her long fingers slowly caressed down Pauline's arms.

"Delilah, it's so good to see you too," Pauline said leaning over to exchange air kisses on either side of her cheeks.

"Who is this?" Delilah said shooting a gaze at Ming.

"This is Ming Mondragon, Delilah. She is the wife of Conrad Mondragon. They've been happily married a very long time. A very long time," Pauline emphasized.

As Pauline made introductions, Delilah's gaze shifted between Ming's face and across the room where Conrad was standing. Her eyes quickly shot back to Ming. She let her gaze slowly take her in. She leaned in close and tilted her head. "You look gorgeous in that dress Ming," she said as she quickly licked her lips. It was evident that Delilah was more than interested in Ming.

The gesture was so quick and subtle Ming was sure Pauline didn't notice it.

Delilah was caught up in her thoughts and didn't hear Pauline. "What did you say, cousin?"

"Cousin?" Ming inquired.

Delilah softly laughed. "Yes."

Pauline cleared her throat. "Yes, didn't I tell you, Ming? Delilah Deauville is a relation of mine, who prefers to call me cousin. Why do you think I know her so well?" she cleared her throat. "Why do you think I told you about Delilah's…ah…Little likings?"

"Cousin, there is no need to provide so much information," Delilah said shaking her head.

Pauline gave a tiny shrug. "We are only related by marriage," she said tersely.

The moment was awkward.

"Oh Ming, it looks like Conrad is eying his favorite and only wife," Pauline said breaking the ice. "I think you should go and visit with your husband. It looks like he misses you."

From a short distance away, Conrad stood in conversation with Jean Baptiste. He looked up and waived his hand in greeting to Pauline. Instantly his eyes shifted their gaze and locked with Ming's.

Pauline waived back to him. "Conrad, Ming needs you," her voice delicately sliced the air.

"Well, I guess I'll get going. It seems my cousin wants to be rude," Delilah said abruptly not waiting for Conrad to make his way over.

"Ming, we need to talk privately," Pauline said reaching out to squeeze Ming's hand. "I'll meet you at the Junior Royal Court, backstage when you drop the girls off," she murmured low. "If I miss you there, I'll wait for you in the lobby by the bell captain's desk."

Ming nodded.

Pauline gave Ming a push in Conrad's direction.

"Delilah," Pauline's voice was tight as she turned and closed the distance between them. She hooked her arm in hers. "I'm sure your cousin Jean will be glad to see you have arrived. I'm sure he needs to have that talk with you about being on your best behavior tonight," she said quickly clasping Delilah's arm and pulling her away. They took a walk across the ballroom.

Ming joined Conrad across the room.

"Who were you and Pauline talking with?" Conrad asked curiously.

"That was Delilah Deauville. Isn't she beautiful," Ming said without a thought? "There was something curious and beautiful about her. I think it was her eyes."

Conrad shook out his thoughts. "Huh, oh yeah she is. But she is not as beautiful as my wife."

Conrad Mondragon leaned over close. His eyes took in the gracefully attractive woman standing across from him. His wife Ming Jefferson-Mondragon was the piece in the puzzle that kept him human. He smiled remembering. Ming had been a beauty queen, Miss Oakland California. He'd been so proud when he watched her receive her crown.

The two of them had grown up together, off of 105th Avenue in the Durant Manor Area of Oakland California. Ming Jefferson was the girl next door. They mixed well. Conrad was half Black and half Spanish with a little German thrown in. He got his last name Mondragon from his Spanish side.

Ming was half Black and half Asian. Growing up, he and Ming stuck together a lot. Kind of like mixed-race kids support team.

Conrad's eyes lingered on Ming's expressive brown eyes. She radiated beauty from deep within her. To everyone who looked at Ming, he was sure they just saw a chic thin looking woman with a shapely, well-proportioned derrière. Her butt was what he'd loved about her most.

Ming's eyes challenged his as if she knew his thoughts. She moved in closer. "Conrad my husband, it looks like I did not quench your thirst this afternoon," she said taking his hand and casually letting it rest on her well-proportioned derrière.

Conrad smiled and focused his gaze on her. Ming's directness was what he loved about her. He squeezed her flesh between his fingers. "Perhaps we can go up to our suite soon. Maybe for a quickie?"

"Husband, you know you only want a blow job and you are lucky it won't mess up my hair. We'll sneak away soon. I promise," she smiled knowingly.

"When?" Conrad gave her butt another squeeze.

"Oh Conrad, you are so naughty," Ming playfully giggled. "Just as soon as I check Mimi and Lucy in at Junior Court. After that, we can go and play. I'm sure Mother Kahina Laveau will watch the girls for me for the rest of the evening."

Music blared out.

"Whew! They're playing our song Conrad!"

Conrad smiled and nodded. The song held deep meaning for him. "I'd like to feel the passion to the point of no return," he sang the words of the song and then pulled Ming into his arms. "Wife, I must have this dance with you," he said leading her to the dance floor in the Regency ballroom.

Chapter 4

Spoiling the Evening ...
  The Nasty People...

Hidden amid a forest of potted plants Monty Wildfire watched the couple on the garden room dance floor. His eyes glistened over with jealousy and envy.

"Monty, what are you doing hiding behind that fern?" Celica Baptiste curiously asked.

He had been fearful that someone might come along and catch him watching the couple on the dance floor. He'd held his cell phone in his hand just in case they did. He pretended to check his messages.

Celica Baptiste wasn't stupid. She was well educated. She glanced across the dance floor. She saw the object Monty had really been looking at earlier.

He stared back at her. "What do you want Celica?" He demanded, not masking his deep annoyance for being interrupted.

Celica recoiled from Monty's sharp words. The smile on her face faded. She recovered quickly. "I was only joking Monty. I guess I forgot you don't like to be teased. Here, I brought you that champagne you wanted."

He took the glass from her hand and put it down. "Please leave

Celica," he scolded.

"You're not going to have a drink with me?" she asked.

"No, I'm busy Celica."

Celica started to protest but she knew it was useless. For the last year, she'd been trying to get Monty's attention. It had only been two months since she got him interested in her. Her face flushed embarrassed, thinking about how she brought that about. Her thoughts raced as she remembered. She had stayed late one night after their board meeting ended. She and Monty had been alone when she brushed real close to him. The next thing she remembered, she tried something she'd seen in the movies. She cupped her hand around his penis and told him she wanted to feel him in side of her.

Just thinking about it made her embarrassed. She'd gotten to get Monty inside of her alright. But it wasn't the way she had wanted. Instead, he had her give him a blow job. She shook herself, thinking how stupid she had been. But then she'd finally figured out how to endear herself to him. The way to get to most men's hearts was to cook for him and feed him. The way to get to Monty's heart was by using money; Monty loved making money. "But you don't know what I did for you...," she hesitated. She smiled and blurted "I've got the opportunity you've been wanting."

Monty lost track of the couple on the dance floor. He lifted a large leaf of the fern and eyed his prey. "Oh really," he said ignoring her.

Annoyed, he turned and glanced back at her. Celica was starting to get on his last nerve. He quickly felt he made a hasty decision agreeing to say she was his date for the evening. As usual, he was sure she hadn't been paying attention to him when he laid down the rule that under no circumstance was she to smother him.

Her eyes widened as she gazed back at him. "You said that if I made things happen for you Monty, we could be something special to each other," she paused. "You know Monty; I consider myself as an obstacles eliminator."

Monty's attention was elsewhere. "Yeah baby, whatever we discussed is fine with me," he mumbled, shifted and turned back around.

Celica's thoughts raced as she thought of what to say to hold his interest. "You know; I've arranged for you to meet him. We can make a lot of money and be something special to each other, just like we said."

His ears perked up at the word money. "Don't play games with me about money Celica. What are you talking about?"

Celica's eyes flashed, realizing Monty's attention was elsewhere. "Nate Trent is here tonight and he wants to meet with you…I mean us, privately, about working a deal."

Nate Trent was on the board of directors at one of Silicon Valley's oldest Foundations. He was good for working a deal. A deal that didn't involve playing by the books. A deal that could make a lot of money.

Monty's face relaxed. He softly smiled. "Where is Nate?"

"What about our being something special to each other Monty?"

"Yeah baby, not to worry. But let's first get the deal going. I want to meet with Nate. Where is he?"

"I'm not sure. I saw him speaking with a woman, earlier in the lobby. I haven't seen him since. But he insisted he will meet with us, here tonight."

What happened next was unexpected.

"Monty, I was hoping to see you," Nate's voice sliced the air.

Nate Trent moved in closer and wedged himself between the two. He stuck out his hand. "Well, how could I refuse to meet with you? Not after your assistant, Celica, brought three bottles of your signature champagne up to my suite," he nodded. "By the way, the bottle I drank was exquisite."

Monty shook his hand enthusiastically. "Well, if you need more, don't hesitate to ask. I have plenty in my suite," his eyes darted back at Celica knowingly.

Celica took the hint. She knew the idea was hers. But she kept quiet.

Nate turned and studied the woman next to him. "Hi Celica, nice turnout tonight. Great event, don't you think?"

"Yes, it is Mr. Trent."

Nate's eyes looked Celica over from head to toe. "You're having a love affair with hot pink I see. The dress looks good on you. You know, not many women can wear the color."

Celica smiled. "Why thank you."

Nate shoved his hands in his pockets. "Well, Celica, how about you run along and get me a drink? It'll give me a moment to talk to Monty privately," he shrugged. "Don't worry, if we set up a meeting date you'll be the first to know."

Celica looked apprehensive. She felt insulted after all her hard work bringing the two men together. But she knew when to ignore rude behavior. "Oh, why yes of course." Her eyes darted back to Monty's before she turned to walk away.

"Oh, huh, I'll have bourbon on the rocks," Nate called after her. He watched until she was out of earshot.

Nate shot a glance at Monty.

A look of amusement passed between the two men.

Nate leaned in close to Monty and chuckled softly. "What's going on with you and that bitch in hot pink? You do know she doesn't look good in pink. But she does give a mean blow job."

Monty chuckled. "So we're finally going to have that meeting Nate?"

"You really want to do business with me don't you Monty?" Nate asked. "So tell me how much is it worth to you?"

"I don't know what you mean," Monty replied, not willing to degrade himself.

"I mean I've watched you, Monty. I know what is of interest to you. What you love," he paused his tone was business like.

Nervously Monty rubbed his chin.

Nate chuckled. "I'm talking about your love affair with money; it's the same as my own. I wouldn't think of trying to put together anything that's less than a quarter of a million. What do you think of that?" he asked.

Monty rubbed his chin. "On that, we agree," he assured him.

Nate adjusted his tie. He ran his hand down the front of his Armani tuxedo. "I can tell a man with tastes the same as my own. That Rolex Daytona you're wearing is rare and beautiful. It's a classic," Nate said admiringly.

Monty smiled. "That it is. You have a great eye."

"I have an excellent eye. You love women and you love making love to women. I can tell," he said as his eyes darted toward the dance floor. "You might be wise to place your eyes and lust elsewhere." He nodded in the direction of Pearl and Louis dancing. "That one is loyal to Louis La Cour. I can tell you that much. And believe me, I've tried."

"Oh?" Monty paused with his thoughts. He felt a surge of anger knowing that Nate had lusted after Pearl La Cour. In the back of his mind he felt like punching him in the face. His jaw tightened as he masked his feelings superbly.

"Not in the way you think. I just tried to be a good friend. Get close to her. Be nice, but she wasn't having any part of it. Pearl La Cour has got values. Morals," he paused. "Anyway, it's best to work on a woman with no moral values. They are the easy ones to get in bed."

Monty sighed softly, realizing it hadn't been what he thought. "I know what you mean."

"Anyway, we will meet soon to discuss details, Monty. But not tonight," Nate said confidently. "After talking about giving a mean blow job I'm in need of one now. And there is a woman here tonight that's willing. It doesn't hurt that she's in the business of giving pleasure."

The two men chuckled.

"Sounds like definitely an easy prey," Monty said.

Nate chuckled softly and then stopped abruptly. "Oh, and by the way, we will conduct our meeting privately, without the hot pink wonder. No need to split our profit into thirds, when we can both have a half."

Monty grinned. "I love the way you think Nate."

Nate pulled himself up to full height and breathed out slowly. "Whew! I need that blow job pretty fierce now and I need to get going if I want to get the black-haired girl. She can make a man feel like a king if you tip her well."

Monty looked up.

"Don't look so taken aback Monty. This is a hotel. Everything can be bought for the right price. Besides, this woman does business here at the hotel all the time. Her girls are well-mannered, genteel and receptive to taking care of details, if you know what I mean. You should look around you more often and observe."

Suddenly Celica walked back carrying Nate's drink.

"Here's your bourbon on the rocks Mr. Trent."

"Ah…Thank you Celica," Nate said, taking the glass out of her hand. "As always, you can be counted on to charm, fetch, retrieve and act dumb," he condescendingly said while walking away.

Chapter 5

Paying a price to live this life...

Pauline Baptiste walked a short distance away from her husband Jean Baptiste. As usual, he'd dismissed her concern that he speak with his cousin Delilah Deauville about her behavior. Now was not the time, Jean had said, as he squeezed her hand. Now was never the time.

Pauline had married Jean Claude Maximille Baptiste when she was twenty-one. Back then, just as now, it cost money to live, and Jean's family had money.He could afford a wife and he could give her father a loan to keep his real estate business going.

There was a price to be paid for that loan to keep her father's business going. There was a price to pay for everything that happened in life.Pauline's eyes eagerly watched her daughter Katrina Baptiste as she strutted brazenly around the room like her cousin Delilah Deauville

Pauline's lips thinned into a frown. She didn't like it when Katrina acted like she was. She had big dreams for her daughter. She wanted her to go to Berkley or Stanford, maybe even Vassar College. She wanted Katrina to marry a good man. A good man like Ming Mondragon had.

Her eyes slanted, focusing, as she watched a young man walk up to Katrina and engage her in conversation. He had reached out possessively and took her hand in his. The handsome young man was Jorge Manteau.

Katrina and Jorge Manteau were both very beautiful. They made a handsome couple.For once she was glad to see him. Jorge was of mixed parentage, and the fact that his father didn't bother to marry his mother no longer was a concern to her.

"Jorge, it is so good to see you. I knew you'd come and see Katrina compete tonight," Pauline's voice delicately rung out as she closed the distance between them.

Jorge Manteau's eyes lit up in surprise as Pauline embraced him in a hug.He felt like he'd been captured by a hunter.

"Mrs. Baptiste, it's so good to see you," he gave her a warm smile back. "I was just telling Katrina I have to leave."

"Oh, I am so sorry to hear that, Jorge. I was hoping you'd keep me company."

"Then I must say I'm sorry again," Jorge replied nervously. "I mean, I would have loved to keep you company this evening. But even though I won't be able to see Katrina in the pageant tonight, I did bring over my father's donation check, in her behalf, Katrina, I mean."

"Really, Jorge, that was so kind of your father," Pauline smiled eagerly, as he eyes flashed greedily. "Did you want to leave his check with me? I will see to it that it gets in the hands of Clare Palling."

"I've already dropped it off," Jorge declared.

"Why, isn't that wonderful," she exclaimed. "Please tell your father I said thank you, Jorge."

"I would be he'd much rather hear if from you and your husband Mr. Baptiste. In fact, he told me to tell you to contact him with a date you and Mr. Baptiste, can come over for dinner."

"Excellent! I will give your father a call," Pauline gushed out.

"Well, I must be off," Jorge said, giving Pauline a final hug.

Pauline exhaled contently as she watched Jorge making his exit. Endlessly her thoughts raced through her mind. *"Yes, there was always a price to be paid for living this life."*

Chapter 6

Wait a minute ...

"Mrs. Palling, can you tell me where I can find Louis La Cour?"

Clare Palling looked up into the gray-green eyes of Jean Baptiste. She folded her arms on her desk as he walked closer.

Jean Baptiste smiled. He'd gone from elementary school through high school with Clare Palling. He knew she was two years younger than he was. She may have been an accountant, but she was very easy on the eyes. Her high cheek-boned face held fathom deep eyes. She'd aged well.

"Do you remember that time you, me, and a few other kids from high school, went downtown to Murphy Street and hung out at the pool hall?"

"Yeah, I remember. We had a lot of fun that night. You and me and that Ravenna Blackstone girl; she was dating Big Fred Bonaparte," she said with a laugh. "We stayed on that pool table for hours, laughing and joking and drinking root beer."

Jean enjoyed watching Clare Palling smile. God, she'd aged well he thought. From the first time, he'd ever seen her, he'd thought she was the one-woman God had given beauty to. Everything about her was prefect, from her thick wavy long hair to a perfect face and body. He

36

reminisced back to their days in school together. She raced through his thoughts and he smiled.

She took a sip of her coffee. She had seen her share of overpriced charity balls in her lifetime. She noted Jean held a plump envelope in his hand. She watched as he put the envelope on the desk in front of her. Tonight's ball wasn't cheap. She knew Jean Baptiste had committed to ten thousand dollars for the table he'd purchased for tonight's dinner. She also thought of the fees he'd paid in advance to have his daughter entered into the Royal Queen Pageant. Being an accountant, she'd seen most people pay for their tickets, fees, donations and such with checks or credit cards. Cash payers were a rarity.

She reached for the envelope and smiled. "Whew, it looks like there's a lot of cash in that envelope. Jean, you've never paid for your event tickets with cash before."

The smile on Jean's face died instantly. Clare Palling was just like his Pauline. Always hungry for his money he thought, as he snatched the envelope from her hands. "Hey, wait a minute that cash is not for my event tickets for tonight. You know I normally just mail you a check."

The moment was awkward.

Clare frowned. What an embarrassing situation. It was obvious to her that Jean was lying. She stared between Jean and the envelope.

Jean hesitated then looked at the envelope. "Ah, oh this," he said, stuffing the envelope back into his jacket pocket. He hoped the lie he was about to tell wasn't evident. "I was just getting some cash out to give Pauline. She wants to buy some raffle tickets later."

Clare leaned across the desk. She stared at him. Her expression was polite but curious. "Raffle tickets with that much cash?" she laughed out. "Well, you must want Pauline to win all of those donated raffle prizes real bad."

Jean's entire mood changed. His smile was tight. "Yes, I do. Pauline has her heart set on winning a prize. Anyway, I'll be mailing in my check as usual for our tickets," he said nervously looking away. "I was looking for Louis. Is he around?"

"No, sorry. Louis is out making the rounds."

Jean shrugged. "You don't have any idea where he is?"

"Well, he could be in the mezzanine on the second floor right off of the Regency Ballroom, or he could be in the Grand Ballroom. It's hard to say."

"Well, I guess I'd better start looking for him."

"Yeah, you do that Jean," she said turning around reaching to refresh her cup of coffee. It was going to be a long night", she thought.

Jean turned slowly and left.

Chapter 7

A little problem...

The little girl stood beside the dance floor, eagerly watching the couple dance. Several times she waived and tried to make eye contact.

The couple dancing ignored her. Finally, the music ended. The man grabbed the woman's waist and pulled her close in a hung. The couple walked off of the dance floor.

"Thank goodness, your dance is over," the little girl hissed out in a tizzy. Her hair looked a mess.

Immediately she ran over and grabbed her mother's hand.

Pearl gazed down at her daughter. "Lacey, what are you doing in the garden room? This room is for adults only."

"Daddy, do you mind if I borrow mom for a moment?"

Louis looked back at his daughter. She was the miniature image of her mother. He smiled proudly knowing his blood line ran though this beautiful little girl. He shook his head knowing what time it was going to take to untangle the mess on her head. He reached and patted his daughter's hair. "Lacey Catherine Kadira La Cour, what did you do to your hair?" He didn't wait for an answer. "Never mind, forget I asked.Your mother will take care of you and that mess in your hair. I need to go and check on the queen pageant. It's about time we got things started."

Lacey watched gratefully as her father walked away.

Pearl surveyed her daughter with loving admiration.

"Mommy, I need you," Lacey said as she spun around and scooted in closer. She pushed her long curly reddish-brown hair behind her ear. "Maëlle Mallard said she could style my hair to look just like Katrina Baptiste. But she couldn't."

"Whew, did she now?" Pearl frowned. She sighed heavily. "Okay, come on Lacey. It's a good thing we booked a suite upstairs. I don't think the San Jose Hotel's Beauty Salon could do a thing with your hair after the famous stylist Miss Maëlle Mallard worked her magic"

Lacey giggled.

Rapidly skittering small footsteps were heard behind them. Lacey glanced quickly behind. She looked anxiously at her mother and said. "Mom, Maëlle really didn't mean to mess up my hair. Can she please come with us?"

Pearl stopped abruptly and turned. "Yes, you can come too, Maëlle."

Maëlle smiled back at Pearl with deep affection. "Thanks Mrs. L."

Pearl led the two girls towards the elevator. They walked past the bar. There sitting at the bar sat her mother in law.

"Grand-mere Catherine," Pearl called out anxiously. "Would you like to come with us? We are on our way up to the suite."

"No," she said reflectively looking at the two little girls standing next to Pearl.

Catherine Marie Rousseau-Andries La Cour was Louis' mother. She was fearless and feisty. She possessed a hidden bold streak that unashamedly reared its head in moments like this one.

She was affectionately and fearfully known as Grand-mere Catherine.

An unspoken accord of shock registered on Lacey and Maëlle's face as they looked directly between each other, then back at the Grand Lady sitting at the bar holding a martini glass.

Grand-mere Catherine looked down at her martini glass and back at the two little girls embarrassed. She sat her glass down and turned around.

"Okay Lacey and Maëlle, you caught your old grandmother having a drink. It's what we old grown folks do from time to time," she fixed her dress. "Nothing to worry about. And since I saw the two of you earlier waiting for Pearl, I knew I was officially off duty. Now you two stay with Pearl. You hear me?"

"Yes, Grand-mere," Lacey and Maëlle said simultaneously.

Pearl looked at her mother-in-law non-judgmentally. "Well, the girls and I were on our way up to the suite. I need to fix Lacey's hair."

Grand-mere Catherine arched an eyebrow. "Yeah you do that Pearl. It needs it badly. Maëlle Mallard, I don't think you should pursue a career in hairstyling. It is not your calling," she said lifting her hand in a mock toast.

Pearl looked at her mother-in-law with a disapproving slant. "Grand-mere Catherine you may want to stop drinking. Aren't you going to babysit the girls after I'm done with Lacey's hair?"

"Oh no, Pearl. Ah MMM not. After the headache those two caused me," she shook her head. "I'm off duty as a baby sister tonight. Mother Kahina Laveau agreed to watch them for the rest of the evening. She's watching the Mondragon girls too. So, they won't be lonely."

Lacey frowned. "Mommy we don't want the warden to babysit us."

Pearl looked simultaneously between Lacey and Maëlle. She shook her head. "Lacey, how many times do I have to tell you, don't call Mother Laveau the warden?That goes for you too Maëlle."

The two young girls looked thoroughly embarrassed.

Grand-mere Catherine's voice coolly said, "Oh Lacey and Maëlle, as soon as Pearl is done with your hair, be quick about getting yourselves to the warden. Mother Kahina Laveau does not like to have to spend her precious time looking for little girls."

Pearl hung her head trying not to laugh. "Come on you two, let's get to our room," she said walking away.

"Mom, do we have to go with the warden?" Lacey asked.

"Lacey don't call her that. Mother Kahina Laveau is a delightful, responsible woman who takes her babysitting duties seriously," she smiled. She knew that Mother Kahina Laveau wasn't going to put up with any of Lacey's or Maëlle's kid foolishness.

Pearl led the two girls to the elevator. She opened her purse and retrieved her card key.Last Saturday night their whole family, including Maëlle, had been home playing Monopoly. For once she missed game night at the La Cour family home.

Chapter 8

Grandmothers and other Holy Things…

A small stout woman stood next to a potted fern. Her dark eyes danced with happiness in her round face. A few strands of gray hair were seen in the part down the middle of her hair. Her thick hair was plaited into a complicated bun at the back of her neck.

Ina Rosolado's eyebrows arched seriously as she inspected her grandson's tuxedo jacket. She flicked off a piece of crumb.

"Quinn Darnell Rosolado Rolandis you look like a Mayan Clark Kent," she said in a heavy Spanish accent.

The young boy standing next to him seemed to be fighting a laugh.

A man walked close. Hello Mrs. Rosolado."

Ina turned and looked up. "Hello Horace. My goodness, you look very handsome in your tuxedo tonight," she shook her head. Her voice was firm. "Boys, see how well, Mr. Horace Garrison looks in his tuxedo. That is why you should keep your jackets on."

Horace looked between the two boys. Quinn and Nicholas had been hard at play.Nicholas still had his coat jacket off and his sleeves rolled up.

Shyly Nicholas peeked up at him. "Hi Mr. Horace."

"Hi Nicholas," he smiled. "From the looks of things, I'm guessing

43

you and Quinn have been playing in the hotel's water fountain again. Here, let me help you put your jacket back on."

Nicholas squeezed close. "Mr. Horace, would you do me a big favor? Don't tell my dad about our playing in the water fountain."

Horace laughed. "Okay Nicholas, I won't tell. But I can't promise you what Mrs. Ina will say."

Nicholas finished buttoning his jacket. "Wow! Thanks Mr. Horace. Quinn already asked Mrs. Ina not to say anything about our being in the water fountain. And she promised she wouldn't. You know Mrs. Ina, Quinn's grandmother, is a really holy thing. She would never tell us a lie or anything."

At that moment Ina Rosolado's eyebrows arched. She winked at Horace letting him know she heard their conversation.

Horace winked back and then put his hand on Nicholas' shoulder. "You know Nicholas, you do look real good with your tuxedo on. Who knows, maybe one of the girls from the Junior Royal Court may see you in your tuxedo and ask you to be their escort?"

Nicholas shrugged and shyly hung his head. "Ah, I'd have to look like royalty or something to get one of them to ask me to be in the Junior Royal Court. I don't have royalty in my blood like you do Mr. Horace."

Puzzled, Horace asked. "What was that Nicholas?"

"My Mom said you had royal blood. She said she knew it was true because you and her both grew up in Goldonna Louisiana. She also said that maybe the two of you shared a cousin or two," he said without pausing. "Anyway, she said you have a rich heritage that is made up of Irish Jamaican Royalty," he breathed out. "I know this because Mom said you had a White Irish Great Grandmother who was royal lady-in-waiting or queen or something royal, right? And she said that we could be related because lots of folks are related to each other back in Goldonna."

Horace thought for a moment, wondering where Nicholas was going with this conversation. "Yes, she was right. What's on your mind then

Nick?"

"I figure, since I look as good as you in my tuxedo and since my mom came from Goldonna, just like you, she might be kin to your royal relatives too. And since my dad and you are best friends, then maybe it would be okay if I tell folks I'm royalty too.

Horace laughed. "Whew, what you just said is really a mouth full Nicholas, but I guess if you want to say that you're related to royalty, it's all right with me."

"Hi Mr. Garrison," Quinn grinned edging closer. "Can I ask you something too?

"Whew, Quinn, I guess so," he said. "Boy I hope it won't be as complicated as what Nicholas just asked me," he thought.

Quinn shook his head. "Ah, don't worry. I just want to know if it's true your middle name is Sherlock? You know like Sherlock Holmes?"

Horace Sherlock Bailey Garrison was a very handsome man. He smiled at the two boys and remembered himself at their age. He decided to give them a little history lesson.

"Yes, but my middle name is also Bailey and the Bailey name is just as important as the Sherlock name. For instance, did you know that I was given the name Bailey so that I would always remember my White Irish Great-Great Grandmother who was royalty? And did you also know I can trace my mixed-race ancestry back to the legacy of my Jamaican roots?"

"I knew that one," Nicholas said. "I also know you got your deep vivid green eyes and jet-black eye lashes from your Irish Great-Great-Grandmother, right?"

Nicholas' statement gave Horace a moment of pause.

"Really? Who told you that?"

Ina's eyebrows arched as she realized she needed to intervene. "Mr. Horace, sometimes the young can talk too much. Don't you think so?"

She turned her gaze back to the boys. "Quinn and Nicholas, you two don't leave my sight, okay."

Horace glanced up at Ina and realized how patient and observant she was. He also noticed something else. "Thanks for taking care of the boys, by the way, if I forgot to mention it. You look very beautiful yourself."

A radiant smile crossed her face. "Oh, I don't mind taking care of the boys. The boys are no problem. In fact, they are always making me laugh when I least expect it."

Horace nodded agreement and turned his attention. "Nicholas, where's your father Louis?

Nicholas shrugged. "I haven't seen dad since we got here. Mrs. Clare Palling, the accountant, met us at the door. Then she and Dad whispered back and forth. Dad told Mom something and he left."

"Where's your mother or your grandmother?"

"Grand-mere Catherine said she was going to go sit at the bar up front and wait for Mom. Mom had to take Lacey up stairs to our suite and fix her hair, he said without taking a breath.

"Well, Mrs. Ina, it's getting close to Junior Court time. I'll leave you now," Horace said walking away.

Ina Rosolado inspected her grandson one more time. "Okay.

Quinn Darnell Rosolado Rolandis, you and Nicholas stay out of trouble. The Junior Court will be assembling soon. No more water fountains, okay my little Mayan Clark Kent?"

Nicholas let out a laugh.

Quinn tilted his head and looked at his best friend standing beside him. "What are you laughing at Nicholas Avoyelles La Cour? Your name is just as long as mine."

Nicholas shook his head. "I'm not laughing at your name Quinn. I'm laughing because your grandmother said you look like a Mayan Clark Kent."

"Very funny," Quinn said.

Chapter 9

Public Television wants an interview...

Louis was whistling a happy tune as he made his way out of the men's room at the San Jose Hotel. He walked down the foyer. He was a man on a mission. He needed to go and check on the pageant and make sure everything started as planned.

"Hey Louis!"

Louis La Cour stopped abruptly and looked up. It was his good friend Horace Sherlock Garrison. "Hey Horace, I'm glad you could make it."

Horace Sherlock Garrison was expertly dressed. His tuxedo was excellently tailored to fit him precisely.

Louis mentally pondered about Horace. He was an old friend. He had that attractiveness that could easily turn a woman's head. And he was a good listener. Louis also knew Horace was the same age as his wife Pearl. They were both ten years younger than him. They had grown up together in Goldonna Louisiana.

Louis gave Horace the once over again and realized he was wearing his press badge. He figured Horace wanted an interview. He knew he worked for a local public television station that also held a radio station and a newspaper.

"Horace, how are things?"

Horace gave a laugh. "Things are fine Louis."

Louis thought of some small talk. "Well good then. So, are you having a good time tonight? Do you need me to show you around? He asked without waiting for an answer. "We've got a lot of festivities set up. There is Casino gaming down the hall in the small ballroom," he said then quickly added. "But all proceeds go to charity as I'm sure you know."

Horace nodded and adjusted his tuxedo jacket. "Yes, I know. But I've got to take care of business right now. Just like you Louis, I'm a man wearing several hats tonight."

Louis grinned. "Well I can understand that. So, what is it that you need?"

"I'm representing KPBS. The television station wants an interview since Grand Isles Foundation received monies from the National Endowment for Social Responsibilities and Humanities.

"Whew, Really?" Louis whistled out.

"Don't tell me you didn't know I'd be here for that reason. I know you Louis. You are always on top of things."

Louis liked the compliment. "Yeah, I knew. Do you just want me to read our press release or do you have other ideas?"

"Kind of sort of both," Horace said and then realized he needed to sell his interview. "Right now, I have the cameraman setting up in front of the huge doors of the main ballroom. That way we can capture the feel of the moment," he said waving his hand. "Then I'll ask you a few questions. This will give a live feel to the interview and show folks in television land how important and popular this event is. After that you read the press release or adlib."

"That sounds good." Louis said.

"Good," Horace said. "Remember, our main objective is to inform people about what the Grand Isles Foundation does in helping the community."

"Okay, then let's do this." Louis said.

Chapter 10

Falling for a Dancer...

"At least the cheap champagne is flowing freely," Celica Baptiste thought as she snagged another glass off of a passing tray. She'd looked high and low for her date, or rather her employer, Monty Wildhorse. It seemed like he'd vanished into thin air.

A few minutes later she glanced around the room again. She sipped her champagne.

A man in a uniform stood out among all of the tuxedos. Perhaps that was why he caught her attention.

She downed half the glass of champagne and looked away. Time seemed to stand still.

"Would you care to dance?"

Holding her glass Celica Baptiste looked beside her. The man in the uniform had closed the distance between them. Her eyes focused on the shiny gold buttons on the man's uniform. She tilted her face up to see the man's face. He was tall, very tall.

"Oh, you were asking me?"

The man nodded. "I don't see another beautiful woman standing here in a pink dress. My name is Rogmar Womack. My friends call me Rog. By the way, you look ravishing," he said.

Celica giggled and looked back at the seriously handsome face. Dark friendly eyes smiled back at her. One thing was for sure, Rogmar Womack was a healthy man who had a strong, muscle toned body that looked like he knew how to service a woman. "Rog, my name is Celica. Celica Baptiste. You look like a very tall prince charming in that uniform."

"Then Prince Charming it is. By the way, I love to dance, so don't be surprised if you start falling in love with a dancer," he said smiling.

A sexy hot salsa beat began to play.

Celica put down her champagne glass. "Rog, you are very smooth and easy on the eyes," her voice was sensually soft. "I've always wanted to meet the one and only Prince Charming who loved to dance.

Suddenly a sultry salsa beat filled the air.

"Come along Rog. I hope you know how to salsa," she said allowing him to steer her onto the dance floor.

An hour later Celica felt oddly attracted to Rog. She eyed him eye-to-eye as their dance ended.

She hadn't danced that sensually with a man in a long time. It was obvious Rogmar Womack had had dance lessons.

Rog rested his hand lightly on Celica's shoulder.

"Thank you for the dance. It was fantastic."

"Dance? Is that what you call what we just did? I'm exhausted."

Rog led them to a cozy sitting area. He watched as Celica sank into a plush comfy chair.

"Are you enjoying yourself?" Rog asked.

"Of course, I am. I haven't danced like this, I mean with a real live person," she paused and looked up at him. "I mean, in my dreams, I always imagined that one day a man and I would dance like that. And, well, it looks like my dream has finally come true."

Rog pinned her with a fascinating gaze. His gaze was mesmerizingly seductive. "You don't have a boyfriend do you?"

"I mean, I'm interested in being your boyfriend, dating you, you know the whole package."

Celica Baptiste swallowed hard. She felt like she was being placed under a spell as she stared back at him. Rog was the picture of what every woman dreamed of. He had muscles, manners and good looks. She shook her head. "No, and I hope you're not married or have a steady girlfriend."

He grinned wide. "No to both, for now," Rog hesitated. "But I am working on the steady girlfriend part. How about we go and have a drink?"

"I would love to, Prince Daddy Long legs," she said, taking his arm.

Chapter 11

A Blast from her past...

Catherine Marie Rousseau-Andries La Cour stood at the end of the ballroom and stared across the room. The dimly lit room afforded her the opportunity to watch them, unnoticed.

She watched the elegantly attired majestic-looking tall man dancing with the woman in the purple satin dress that was cut low in the front. The woman looked good for her age. But Catherine knew her. When you stood up close, the woman had fine lines around her eyes that gave her age away.

Catherine also knew the woman was much older than the man.

The dance ended abruptly, and the lights grew bright quickly. The man nodded his head at the woman and walked away. She watched him snag a glass of champagne off of a passing tray.

All at once his dark eyes looked up and locked with hers. He closed the distance between them instantly. She felt like he was looking right through her.

"Catherine Marie Rousseau-Andries La Cour," he exhaled slowly. "The only woman I've ever loved that wouldn't marry me," he stared at her.

"Remington Breaux, I thought I spotted you earlier," her voice softened, as she scanned the room nervously. She wondered if anyone was watching the two of them together. "What are you doing here?"

"Catherine, have you forgotten? The annual Grand Isles Christmas Ball brings together company CEO'S, Presidents, as well as major donors and investors to raise money for a worthy charity," he said. "Besides I received a personal invitation signed by your son, Louis La Cour."

"Oh, did he now?"

"Gosh, you are still beautiful. I spotted you when I first arrived. You were watching your granddaughter. You looked so happy, I couldn't take my eyes off of you," he smiled.

Catherine's eyes brightened at his words. She stared back at him. Remy was still a handsome good-looking man with broad shoulders and a hard chest. He looked handsome dressed in his tuxedo.

"Remy, I see you still have charm and talent in great abundance," she shook her head. "You know that charm of yours just keeps getting better and better every year."

He chuckled softly. "For all the years I've known you Catherine, you are the only woman I let call me Remy. It makes me very happy when you do," he teased.

Catherine prided herself on her judgment of character. Remy had been the only man she'd ever misjudged. After she'd been widowed for a couple of years, Remington Breaux had come back into her life. She had dismissed him, thinking that he was only interested in her because of the large share of stock she held in a company that Remy and her deceased husband had owned together. Their disagreement had gotten out of hand. It was so bad that she had even involved her son Louis in their disagreement. A year later, she learned that she had been wrong, but by then Remy had left town. She never got a chance to apologize. She regretted it dearly.

Feeling her eyes on him, Remington glanced up and caught her staring. She quickly averted her gaze. She scanned the room realizing her son Louis might see her. Feeling Remy's eyes on hers she looked up.

A twinkle was in his eyes. He chuckled amusedly. "I hope you're not scoping out other men while you're standing here with me," he teased her.

Catherine laughed. "I forgot what a charmer and a tease you are Remy.If you keep pouring the charm on me like that Remy, I may need to talk with you somewhere in private," she teased.

"I love it that you still have a sense of humor," he grinned playfully. "Then, I will continue to charm you my dear," his voice grew serious."Because the truth must be said that I only came here tonight with the hope of seeing you and now," he hesitated. "I'll do or say whatever it takes to keep you talking to me. I've never gotten over you Catherine. Never," he flashed a loving wicked smile.

Catherine exhaled deeply and scanned the room again nervously. She reached out and took Remy's arm. "Gosh Remy, you are a handful. I'm never bored with you. That is for sure. Come, we need to take this conversation somewhere private."

She took his arm and led the way out of the ballroom and across the hotel's foyer. They walked arm in arm outside into the dimly lit patio garden.

As soon as Catherine realized they were alone in the gardens she turned toward him and stepped in close. She felt lightheaded; she was sure it was because of all the champagne she had been drinking. She raised her head and brushed her mouth across his, drawing him into a kiss.

She pulled out of his embrace and looked back at him. Quickly, she tried to think up small talk to cover up what she'd just done. "It's a great ball, wouldn't you say Remy?"

Remy nodded. "It's a fantastic party. I, for one, am enjoying myself. He reached down and his soft fingers traced her cheek. Slowly his hands grasped the side of her face and drew her in for an intoxicating kiss.

Catherine trembled from his touch. She murmured as he kissed her again. "I'm so glad you are enjoying yourself, Remy. I'm so glad you are here. I have always wanted to apologize for that night."

For a moment Remington Breaux was completely still. "Shhhhh Catherine it's okay. God, I've missed holding you," he murmured. Then his hands slid down encircling her and pulling her close.

There was a sound of rustling brushes and movement in front of them in the hedge. All at once a skinny young man with ruffled mussed up hair burst through the hedge. He reached back and pulled a girl though the hedges. She giggled and her eyes grew wide in her face.

"Sorry for interrupting…Your affair," the wide-eyed girl giggled out, as the two trotted off to find another hiding place.

Catherine pulled out of Remy's embrace. Her voice rising. "My God, what am I doing standing in the moonlight kissing you like I'm some high school kid?"

"Catherine, please calm down," he said grabbing her hand. He looked her in the eyes. "You worry too much about what other people think. Those two kids were trying to do exactly what we were doing. Only we're both grown adults who have every right to do what makes us happy."

She hesitated. "I guess you're right. I am happy being with you tonight Remy. It's just that…"

A chill of dread went through Remy. "It's just what? Catherine, I found you again. I want to be with you. I can feel you want to be with me too."

"Oh, Remy I do," she shook her head. "It's just that I don't want to be discovered this way. I mean, I wish we could be together somewhere alone and private where we can talk and be alone."

His face beamed with enthusiasm. "Oh really? What if I told you I have a suite booked here tonight at the hotel? And every night if you want me to."

"Do you really? Here at this hotel?" Catherine asked.

"Yes. Come go there with me," Remy said.

Catherine paused. She breathed out slowly. "I want to. But I can't right now.

Irritation and sadness flashed in his eyes.

"No Remy, I just mean I want to make sure we are not disturbed. I must first make sure my daughter-in-law knows I can't watch my granddaughter tonight, that's all. We already had a baby-sitter lined up. I can meet you in your suite, right after I double check things."

Remington Breaux looked pleased with her answer. "Then you'll meet me at my suite," he said checking his watch. He reached inside his jacket."Here's my room key card. I'll get another one at the front desk. I'll see you just as soon as the pageant is over."

Catherine caught Remington's eye. They stared at each other with a mutual understanding that needed no words.

"Yes, right after they have the junior pageant. I'll make my excuses and stay the night with you," she nodded and then smiled wickedly. "I want to see if you've still got that old magic I fell in love with."

"Oh Catherine, you've made this old man happy. I'll be waiting for you my love."

Chapter 12

Sisters bonding, exes and other riddles...

Someone touched her arm. "Sister, I've been looking for you everywhere," a delicate deep drawl floated on her voice. "Hiding out in the bar, are we?"

Catherine Marie Rousseau-Andries La Cour smiled and looked up into grey eyes as deep as her own. She swirled her glass in her hand. Her sister's voice always reminded her of their Cane River Louisiana Creole roots.

"As you see my precious sister," she drawled out slowly.

Catherine had always thought that when her sister Delta Dawn Allemande smiled her prettiness took on a beauty that made people take notice. Her rich curly dark russet brown hair was styled to frame her face. They both had inherited their gray eyes and slender build from their mother.

"Delta, I thought I saw you dancing with that distinguished looking gentleman, Professor Percy?"

"Professor Percy Newhouse is an intellectual bore," Delta said as she opened her evening bag and retrieved her lipstick.

As Delta gripped her evening bag, Catherine noticed Delta's jungle red fingernails matched her evening gown.

Catherine took hold of her sister's hand and inspected it. "I love the red fingernails Delta. They make you look like a queen, ready to conquer the world."

"I thought so too sister. But that stupefied Geek King snob, Percy, told me I was wearing too much red," she said applying lipstick. "Can you believe the nerve of that man?"

"Did he really?" Catherine tilted her head to the side so that her sister couldn't see her smile. "I thought you really liked him?

"No," she hesitated. "Well maybe a little. But the guy talks about himself all the time. He is such a complete bore," Delta said.

She shook her head and patted her sister's arm affectionately. "Catherine, I like the way you styled your hair tonight," she said checking out her hair style in the mirror behind the bar. "I shouldn't have cut my hair this short. Maybe men don't find it an attractive style on me."

Catherine shook her head. "Spare me the self-pity tonight my precious sister. We both know you are beautiful," she said, her voice trailing off. She turned and waived at the bartender.

Delta knew when to change the subject. "What are you drinking?"

"A martini, extra dry," Catherine said nodding her head.

The bartender walked over and took their order.

"I'll have one also," Delta said. She turned and stared at her sister questionably. "Well, Catherine, I'm picking up the vibe that you've got man trouble. I've only known you to take a few drinks when men are involved."

"Of course, I have sister," Catherine's voice drawled.

"Is it someone I know?" Delta asked tentatively. She studied her sister's face. The frown that settled across her face told her a lot.

Catherine gulped down her drink.

Delta's thoughts raced. Then her eyes glazed over in recognition. Her face registered. She frowned. "Say, wasn't that Clive Jemison I saw you dancing with earlier?"

Catherine just stared straight ahead. Her thoughts raced. Delta hadn't seen her with Remington Breaux. If she had she would had mentioned it. Now she was glad she had danced with Clive Jemison. He made a wonderful diversion. She smiled with her thoughts.

She played with her empty glass and studied the mirrored mural behind the bar. The attractive chic décor could keep the eyes occupied for a long time.

The bartender came back with their drinks.

Delta held her tongue until he walked away.

"Catherine. You haven't answered my question. Was that Clive I saw you dancing with earlier?"

Her sister's eyes shot up at her.

"Yes, I did dance with Clive." Catherine said.

"That weasel has the nerve to show his face. I should find Louis and tell him to kick his ass," Delta snapped.

"No!" Catherine said. "Now Delta, get that temper of yours under control."

"But sister that first classed prick cheated on you."

Catherine shrugged. "No, he did not. We were not dating steady at the time," she shook her head. "I didn't give him a commitment that we would be exclusive. The man had a right to date whomever he pleased."

"Gosh Catherine, you really don't sound like you were interested in Clive. I can tell by your voice what you're saying is true."

Catherine sipped her drink. She thought about Clive for a moment. She remembered a conversation the two had had about Delta. Her thoughts were purely selfishly motivated. She smiled knowing her scheme would keep Delta occupied for the rest of the evening, if she told her. She cleared her throat. "Sister, what if I told you a secret? About Clive I mean."

"What? I'm all ears," Delta said curiously.

"Do you want to know the real reason why I was never interested in Clive Jemison?"

"Yes," Delta grinned leaning in close.

"Well, Clive and I never hit it off because once when he was drunk, I asked him if he was interested in dating my baby sister.

Delta almost choked on her drink. "But..." her voice was desperate. "I didn't...I never gave the man any encouragement."

"Oh, don't worry about it Delta. I got Clive drunk on purpose. I always thought his eyes roamed toward you every time you entered the room. I got Clive drunk and then asked him to tell me the truth and he did."

"Why are you telling me this?" Delta asked.

"Well, I figured Clive Jemison is here tonight alone because he was obviously hoping to see you. And because I figured that since you're just not into that boring Professor Percy Newhouse, then maybe you ought to spend the rest of the evening maybe getting to know Clive better."

Delta giggled. "I love the way that mind of yours works sister. Do you really think I have a chance with Clive?"

"Oh, I think you do," she said peering over Delta's shoulder. "In fact, don't look now but Clive Jemison is headed our way."

"Hello Catherine and Delta," Clive said as he walked over. He stood directly in front of Delta.

Nervously Delta gulped down her drink.

"Delta you look exquisite in that evening gown. Red is your color," Clive said nervously. "Would you like to dance with me?" He asked eagerly stretching out his hand.

Delta giggled. "Yes, I would Clive."

The man flushed.

"Have fun you two," Catherine called out as they walked away.

Minutes later Pearl checked her hair in the chic mirror behind the bar. Staring into the mirror she had a direct view of the elevators across the foyer. Her eyes caught a man standing in front of the elevator. The sight of him gave her pause. She swallowed hard.

The man reached out and grabbed the woman's butt.

"What the hell," she muttered under her breath.

A strange feeling came over her. She watched the man silently in the mirror's reflection. He was behaving like a horny oversexed ass.

She tossed back her drink.

Chapter 13

The man marveled as the woman's long jet-black hair fell over her face as her lips did pleasurable things to him.

The room was pungent from a strong aphrodisiac. The rich smell of amber, sandalwood and jasmine made the senses reel.

"Oh God, that feels delicious," Nate Trent moaned. He moved her hair behind her head. Then let his hand reach down to cup her breast.

The petite full chested girl performed her ministrations to the fullest detail. She took great care to heighten his sexual pleasure until his body reached its climatic fever. Minutes later sweat beads of ecstasy poured down Nate's face as his eyes glistened over in happiness.

Nate Trent opened his eyes just as the girl slithered off of his body, out of the bed, and headed for the door. The door opened before she reached it.

"Are you pleased Mr. Trent?" a woman said as the girl slipped through the open door.

"Oh Ms. Lemieux very much so." Nate rose and climbed off of the bed.

"Good. I would hate for you to be displeased. A powerful and very rich man such as you should always have his pleasure as he pleases,"

Ms. Lemieux said.

Ms. Lemieux said all the things she knew he wanted to hear as she watched him with an observant eye. It gave her power and control.

Nate retrieved his clothes. "My only disappointment is that you keep a firm watch on your girls," he buttoned his shirt.

Ms. Lemieux smiled softly and came straight to the point. "You got what you paid for Mr. Trent. It was all you asked for. If you desire more, I can charge your account."

"No, I'm good. Lips do relieve the tension," he interrupted. "Perhaps next time I will require more," he nodded, straightening his clothes and heading for the door.

Ms. Lemieux followed him through the door. She walked him down the hall to the main door of the suite.

Nate stopped abruptly as he reached the main door. He turned and inclined his head. "Ms. Lemieux, until next time," he said closing the door behind him.

Ms. Lemieux made sure the door was locked securely behind him. "You cheap bastard," she mumbled under her breath as she closed the door.

The girl with the long black hair said softly. "Madame Lemieux? Can Tammy Faye and I order from room service now?"

"Of course, you can Duchess. Order whatever you like," she said.

Duchess Lanchow brushed her glossy black hair. It caught the light. Her slanted exotic eyes smiled warmly. "Was he our last client?"

"Yes, in fact after we are all finished eating, you and Tammy Faye can have the rest of the night off."

Chapter 14

The Perceptive Watcher...

Pearl tided up the mess Lacey and Maëlle had left on the bathroom counter. Toothpaste, toothbrushes, and hair ornaments had been thrown all over the countertop.

Pearl finished her task and breathed a sigh of relief. She stood in front of the mirror adjusting her hair.

There was a knock on the door. She prayed it wasn't Mother Kahina Laveau, tired of the girls already. She walked quickly to the door.

Pearl couldn't believe her eyes.

Monty Wildfire's handsome face stared back at her.

"Pearl, may I come in?"

Without waiting for a response, Monty moved smoothly and quickly through the open door.

Pearl's throat tightened. "Monty, I beg your pardon. But I was just on my way back down to the ballroom."

"There's no hurry Pearl," Monty's voice said with laughter. "The competition hasn't started. Besides, I want to give you something."

Pearl's face was grim. After a moment's hesitation she closed the door and followed him into the suite.

"What a lovely room," Monty said strolling around. "The suites at the San Jose Hotel are rich and elegant," he said, as his gaze looked curiously around.

"Yes, they are," she agreed.

Monty walked over and sat down on the sofa. "Hmmm, the Penthouse Suite has some great views. Louis always had great taste."

Annoyance flashed in her eyes. She thought his stare was done to pass judgment."You are assuming I didn't pick this suite. Do you think I lack taste?" Pearl wondered why she was encouraging Monty in conversation.

Monty smiled back at her and said nothing. It was easy to look at Pearl. She was what they called very easy on the eyes. In fact, he found the agitated frown on her face amusing and sexy. He'd bet she had no idea how beautiful she looked right now.

"I'm sorry Pearl, I didn't mean to say you didn't have good taste," he said as his eyes rested tenderly on her face. His eyes charmed her. His voice held a seductive, gentle, kind, commanding tone, which was very effective on the opposite sex. "In fact, I'm sure your taste is just as classy and sophisticated as you are."

Pearl listened to Monty's low sexy seductive voice. He was a charmer. He had the kind of voice that could lead a woman into a world of distress.

"Damn", she said in her thoughts. It was hard not to like Monty. He was the king of flattery. His considerate and kind nature, not to mention his smooth words and good manners, could take a woman's breath away.

"You said you wanted to show me something Monty."

Monty smiled back at her with a disguised admiration. He'd spent weeks thinking of a project that would excite Pearl. He rose from his seat, pulled the envelope from his breast pocket and walked over and handed it to her.

He stood close and folded his arms. He could smell her perfume. It was intoxicating. He breathed deeply, savoring her.

Pearl took the letter and read it in silence. After the first paragraph she turned and gazed at Monty in shock. The voice inside her head started laughing. She turned and continued reading the letter as a smile slowly crept across her face. The proposal listed the Silicon Valley Blanket Food Foundation specifically as the recipient of all donations. It was the foundation Pearl had founded.

She cleared her throat. "Monty you do realize this proposal gives me authority to conduct our joint partnership. And it lists me as Director and Chairman President?" She read further. The letter also stated the foundation would receive a fifty-thousand-dollar starter amount to get things going. Before she knew it she giggled out loud."And it puts me in charge of the budget?"

"I wouldn't have it any other way," he said. "It's a fine foundation that has long been overdue on being noticed.

Pearl could not believe her eyes. Her breath caught in her throat. As she continued and finished reading the letter.

Suddenly she threw her arms around Monty. "Thank you Monty!"

Monty held Pearl tight.

Pearl swallowed hard when she realized he wasn't letting her go. She stiffened in his grip and pushed back to look up at him. "What do you want Monty?" she asked gazing back at him.

Monty didn't answer. He seemed to have trouble breathing. He stared back at Pearl with a glassy gaze. His mouth opened.

Suddenly without seeming to move he grabbed Pearl's arm and pulled her close to him. His lips sought hers.

Pearl struggled. "Let me go Monty!"

"Monty Wildfire get your hands off of Pearl!" Grand-mere Catherine's voice sliced the air. Her icy gray stare held Monty Wildfire's gaze.

The moment was awkward.

"Evening Grand-mere Catherine," Monty said innocently. "Pearl and I were just talking. Weren't we Pearl?"

"I am not your grandmother Monty," Catherine declared.

Monty looked at her and shook his head.

Grand-mere Catherine stared curiously at Pearl. Her steel gray eyes took in the situation.

Pearl didn't reply. She felt embarrassed.

"Look Catherine, I don't know what you think you saw," Monty said before being abruptly interrupted.

"That's Mrs. Catherine Marie Rousseau-Andries La Cour to you Monty!" She bellowed without taking her eyes off of him. And if that's lost on you, then call me Mrs. La Cour!"

Monty shot a cold stare at her.

"I am not a fool Monty, that didn't look like talking to me. It looked like you thought you could do more than talking," her lips tightened.

Monty frowned and lowered his gaze.

Grand-mere Catherine didn't flinch. "You can't even look me in the eye when I'm talking to you." Her hostile gaze stared back at him. "Your good looks and smooth words may help you whore around with any woman that you choose Monty. But my daughter-in-law has good taste. She would never stoop low and have an affair with a man like you Monty. You aren't good enough for a La Cour woman," she uttered abruptly.

Monty raised his gaze and nodded knowing he'd met his match. He swallowed hard. "Look, I'm sorry Mrs. La Cour."

Grand-mere Catherine tilted her head. "Now Monty I have one other thing to correct you on. You are standing too close to my daughter-in-law, and I would feel better if you would move away slowly." She said opening her purse as if intending to take something out. "In fact, don't you have some place you need to be? And if that is lost on you, just know that you need to leave now!"

Her threatening gaze wasn't lost on Monty. He shrugged his shoulders as he watched her keep her hand in her purse. "As a matter of fact, Mrs. La Cour, I was just leaving."

Grand-mere Catherine gazed back at him. "Oh, Monty just one more thing before you go. There's an old saying. You should beware of the watcher. For the Watcher is very perceptive and she always sees."

Monty wrenched his eyes from Grand-mere Catherine's gaze. "Well, Mrs. La Cour, I would say it has been nice meeting you. But that would be a lie."

Before she could say anything else, he quickly made his way to the door.

He glanced up. "Pearl it's been good to see you as always," he said before slamming the door as he left.

"Grand-mere Catherine I don't know what to say," Pearl said.

"Hush child," Grand-mere Catherine exhaled slowly. "I don't want to talk about this. I know you love my son Louis."

"But..."

"Shhhhh, notice the time. Come on Pearl we need to get back to the ballroom, they should have started the junior pageant march by now."

Pearl realized she was still griping the letter from Monty. Slowly she flashed a smile. "I hope you don't mind, but I need to freshen-up. I'll make it quick okay Grand-mere Catherine?

"Oh no child, I don't mind."

Chapter 15

Junior Royal Court...

"Shut up Mimi!" Lucy whined. "And stop laughing at me. Yuck! Your breathe stinks."

"Well, you wouldn't know that if you didn't stand right up in my face, now would you yuck face?" Mimi fiercely laughed making a mean face.

"Mimi looks stupid," Lucy chanted laughing uncontrollably.

"Stop laughing at me Lucy!" Mimi yelled fretfully.

"If you want me to stop laughing at you then stop looking so funny. Funny girl, stupid funny girl," Lucy chanted between giggles.

Mimi glanced at her mother Ming to make sure she wasn't paying attention. All at once she reached over and pinched Lucy's arm.

"Ouch," Mother Mimi pinched me.

Mimi played with her hands. "Uh ah, no I didn't," she shrugged. "And besides you pinched me first."

Ming Mondragon turned around, squared her shoulders and faced her daughters. "Look, I don't care who pinched whom. Stop it both of you," she cried. Sometimes she felt all she did was play referee to her two daughters. Her affection for her daughters was as genuine as any mothers could be. But her patience was wearing thin. Like any mother, she often craved a break from her kids.

"Lacey and Mimi Mondragon, I have been patient with the two of you all day. Mommy needs a break," Ming sighed. "Your antics are starting to get on my nerve. Why can't the two of you be more like your cousin Jade?"

Jade Mondragon was Ming's niece. She was two years older than Mimi her eldest. But unlike Mimi and Lucy, Jade was always a well-behaved and respectful child."If the two of you don't stop. I'll tell Jade you were both acting like two-year olds," she added.

Ming always held Jade's perfect behavior up as an example to her daughters. She held out hope they would both, one day, follow Jade's example of how she expected them to behave.

The two sisters glanced between each other with remorse expressions covering their face.

Ming smiled. Her idol threat had produced the effect she'd hoped it would.

The only other person she could threaten her daughters with to make them behave was Mother Kahina Laveau. She thought with a smile. Tonight, after the ball was over, Mother Kahina Laveau will provide a slumber party for the children. It made her glad.

Ming smiled. Her threat had worked. "Come along girl's Mother Kahina Laveau is waiting."

The two girls were instantly silent.

"Ahhhh," they moaned grudgingly in unison.

They stared at each other simultaneously.

"No!" Lucy whined, her eyes pleading. "You're going to make us spend the night with the warden, aren't you?"

Mimi stared back quietly. She opened her mouth and then closed it quickly. It was obvious she didn't want to try her mother's patience any further.

"Well, girls, I guess you'll just have to wonder. Come along now. Mother Laveau is head of the Junior Royal Court this year. We don't want to keep her waiting."

"She's the head of it every year," Mimi mumbled under her breath, as she followed behind her mother.

Children chatted in small excited groups as Ming entered the backstage area set up for the Junior Royal Court.

"Look, there's Ann and Elizabeth Songbird," Lucy yelled.

"Mom can we go visit with them," Mimi's voice rang out like a song.

"I have to check you both in with Mother Kahina Laveau," Ming said clearing her throat.

Mother Kahina Laveau's voice sliced the air. "Ming don't worry. I can see them both. I have them accounted for," she said.

"If you are in a hurry you can just leave."

Ming nodded. "If you are sure you don't need me to stay."

Mother Kahina Laveau gave Ming a stern gaze. "I've been doing this for years. Plus, it's time we ran through a quick rehearsal."

At that moment Mary Mackey, Mother Kahina Laveau's daughter entered with Lacey La Cour and Maëlle Mallard in tow.

Ming nodded her greeting as she nudged her daughters into the room and quickly made her escape. "Thanks Mother Kahina Laveau and its good to see you Mary," she said.

Mary Mackey nodded and returned her greeting. She cleared her throat and turned and gazed up. "Mother Laveau, here are two more participants in the Junior Court."

Lacey and Maëlle acknowledged Mother Laveau respectfully.

"Okay girls go on and play with your friends. Take Mimi and Lucy with you," she commanded cheerfully.

The children squealed with delight.

"Oh, Mimi and Lucy, your cousin Jade Mondragon is already here," she hastened to add. "We will start lining up with escorts for the Junior Royal court shortly and run through a quick rehearsal."

Mother Laveau waited a moment until the girls were out of earshot. She turned and stared at her daughter. "Mary, did you get Pearl's permission for the girls to attend the slumber party?"

"Yes," Mary said. "Pearl said it was okay. In fact, the girls were asking if we'd hired the same Magician as last year."

Mother Laveau shook her head. "No, thank goodness. That fellow couldn't find his rabbit. We still don't know what happened to that poor animal," she sighed. "The fellow I hired this year does the family cruise ship to Atlantis each year. He's good. Really good," she laughed. "There won't be any lost rabbits this year."

Chapter 16

The Crush ...

Twenty minutes later, Ming dashed for the elevator and made her way to her suite. She opened the door and stepped across the threshold.

She heard soft music playing. "Sweet, sweet sticky thing. Sweet, sweet sticky thing...."

"Conrad, I'm here!" she hollered as she entered. Quickly she dashed down the hallway into the master bedroom. Seconds later Conrad emerged from the bathroom.

"Ming, I've been waiting for you darling" he smiled seductively dropping his towel.

He walked naked over to the bureau and picked up a drink.

Ming stood staring openly, transfixed at how sexy he looked. She thought she was the luckiest woman in the world. This sexy Adonis God was her husband, she said in her mind. She was aroused just staring at him.

"You look tense, Ming. I know how demanding the girls can be. I'm sorry I didn't help you with them earlier," he said. "Here, I made your favorite drink."

"A Toasted Almond, just like I like it. Apology accepted," Ming said, smiling and taking the drink. Conrad is always doing things to make me happy. He loves me so much, she thought.

"Thank you, Conrad."

"You know you are the most important person in my life. I've got to keep my woman happy," he added. "Now drink up," he said clinking glasses.

He downed his drink then watched as Ming's throat rippled, as she swallowed.

She shivered and then smiled. "Whew! That went down smoothly."

Instantly Ming thought she saw a flash of light. She listened attentively. The lyrics of the song that was playing intensified.

Sweet, sweet sticky thing…Sweet, sweet sticky thing. Filled the room.

"Damn Conrad, you look so good standing naked before me. Just like a dream," Ming murmured, her head felt like she had entered a dreamlike haze.

Conrad reached out and pulled her into a close embrace. His lips twitched as he stared back at her. He leaned closer and kissed her and felt her mouth open in response to him.

Abruptly he pulled away pushed Ming out of his embrace. His fingers quickly embraced the zipper of her dress and slid it down.

Ming stepped out of her dress. She stood before him in her black bustier. She still wore her high heels.

Ming watched Conrad's hawk slanted eyes gaze back at her like a predator owning its prey.

He kissed her eagerly this time. It unleashed a groan from Ming's throat.

"Keep the heels on. You look so sexy in them," he murmured and let his lips capture hers. Then his tongue snaked out and eased to her ear. "You are my woman. You do as I say."

Ming groaned at the softness of his voice. It created a delirium of seductive sensual longing. It sent her senses reeling. She relaxed against him astonished at the frantic need to feel him closer.

The kiss went on and on. Then Conrad's mouth wandered to her neck and her shoulders. He thrust his hand inside her bustier and squeezed her breast.

Ming moaned again unable to control her feelings of pleasure. "Oh...I feel warm all over. Damn, I want you Conrad."

"You're feeling your passion. That's good, I love to see a woman enjoying her passion," he said pushing her down on the bed. "You're so beautiful Ming."

Ming felt like her mind was leaving her body. A moment of surprise registered. Her voice was a soft whisper, as her words tumbled out. "Conrad did you put something in my drink? Why? You know I'd do anything for you."

He kissed her softly. "Yes, I know you'd do anything for me Ming, because you love me," he murmured.

"Yes, I love you," she moaned.

Ming, you said you had the courage to do anything. Anything I asked you to do. Don't you remember?"

Ming's eyes grew wide. She knew what Conrad meant. She'd seen that look before. Conrad was bored with her sexually. It didn't matter how many times she went down on him. He'd always felt that maybe he'd missed out on something by marrying Ming so young.

She stared terrified back at him. "Don't...Don't you still?"

"Don't even say that Ming. You know I still love you. I just want us to spice things up a bit," he smiled.

She felt the drug relax her more. She felt like she didn't want to ask any more questions. She thought she felt a soft set of hands caressing her body. She looked back.

Ming's body shuddered. "What's happening Conrad? I feel something strange."

Conrad ran his hand down her face. "Why Ming you're feeling pleasure and more pleasure. Feel it. Let your body flow with it."

"Pleasure, pleasure and more pleasure," Ming mumbled incoherently.

"Yes, I need pleasure and more pleasure in our relationship," Conrad urgently pleaded. "Give me more pleasure," he groaned.

Ming moaned feeling her body relax. "There is someone else here with us isn't there?"

"Yes, Ming you remember Delilah Deauville?"

An intense sensual longing flashed in Delilah's eyes. "Hello again Ming," she said in a hoarse whisper. "I've always had a crush on you."

Ming's body rode a wave of pleasure as Delilah ran her hands down her body. She slowly breathed out. "You have?"

The last thing Ming consciously remembered was Delilah's face as she leaned over and kissed her.

Chapter 17

Confessions, Mixing Love & Pleasure...

Monty Wildfire marched down the hall to the elevator. He was mad as hell. "Who does that old bat, Grand-mere Catherine, think she is? I'm Monty Wildfire. I can have any woman I want," he murmured as he got on the elevator. He punched the buttons without a thought. His handsome face was deeply marred with a frown.

The elevator door slid open.

"Monty Wildfire!" A woman's sultry voice called as she entered.

Monty couldn't recall the voice. His eyes had trouble looking at the woman's face. His eyes locked, spellbound and at eye level with the woman's chest. Forty double D cups gave him a high salute and shook him out of his melancholy mood.

"Admiring the girls Monty?"

Monty nodded and finally looked at the woman's face. It was Fleur Lemieux. Grinning, he rubbed his chin.

Fleur Lemieux was a very tall, very attractive, well-built woman. A man could get lost in her well-built chest.

Unbeknownst to but a few of the wealthiest people in Silicon Valley, Fleur Lemieux ran an escort service. They did more than just make the best looking, eye candy, model types to be escorted to that special event. They could take care of a man's or a woman's every need.

"Well…Well," Monty said approvingly licking his lips. "Are you staying at the hotel Fleur?"

Fleur would be a perfect diversion for the evening, and she would take his mind off of Pearl. He swallowed hard. Damn, Pearl didn't know how much he cared about her. How much he loved her. He stared back at Fleur. He did love her breasts. He licked his lips. Plus, he knew Fleur owed him big time. He'd sent several rich guys her way for business.

"Yes…Yes…Monty I am. If you've got any free time, I can take care of that favor I owe you," she said.

"Well, I won't lie. I'm free now," Monty said.

"How wonderful," she said smiling softly. "It just so happens I'm free right now too. Would you like to do me for free?"

Monty chuckled at her play on words. He was glad the elevator was empty.

"You know I would," he licked his lips again. He could feel his body warming in all the right places.

Fleur pushed the elevator button. The door opened. "This is my floor," she said leading the way to her suite. She walked over to a door and instantly her hand swiped the key card and the door opened.

"Nice," Monty grinned and walked further into the room, admiring the view. The room wasn't as luxurious as the one Pearl was staying in. Funny, he thought he couldn't shake Pearl from his thoughts. He knew why. It was because he wanted her. He wanted Pearl badly. Grand-mere Catherine's words echoed through his mind. She thought Pearl was too good for him. He smiled softly. He figured out a way to show them. He'd get even with La Cour's if it was the last thing he did.

He turned and looked at Fleur. She was tall, yes. But she was nothing compared to Pearl. Still, if he looked at Fleur just right, she didn't look like a whore. He could fuck her with pleasure. He smiled softly.

Fleur Lemieux closed the distance between them. She touched Monty's arm. "I have a full bar set up in the bedroom this way. What would you like to drink?"

"Bourbon, straight," he said.

Monty watched Fleur walk to the bar and pour two glasses of bourbon.

Fleur tried to make small talk. "So Monty, I hear the Grand Isles Ball has already received over four hundred fifty thousand dollars in donations tonight. Do you think this has been the highest amount collected?" she asked running a finger gently against his thigh.

"No, but the final receipts have been calculated. The totals won't be known until at least the end of the week. But the money is for charity. It's all going to a good cause."

Fleur took the moment and unzipped her dress. It fell to the floor. She stood naked before him.

Quickly Monty tossed back his drink and swallowed hard. He reached and poured himself another one. He gulped it down immediately.

He turned around and looked at Fleur. The booze was starting to make her look better.

"Good, no underwear," he said with a shrug. "I hate the stuff; it just slows you down."

Fleur closed the distance between them. "You know, if you think about it, what I'm doing right now is for a good worthy charitable cause too," she said quickly taking off Monty's jacket. Like a skilled pro she unbuttoned his shirt and removed the rest of his clothes in seconds.

Softly he smiled looking down as his body swelled. Seductively he glanced up at Fleur. "You know, the charity you're about to take care of is for a worthy cause too."

Monty's hands went instantly to cup her breasts. His fingers were expert at touching a woman. "I'm going to name your breasts Charity, for they do perform a worthy cause," he murmured as his mouth closed around one of her nipples.

She purred.

Suddenly he felt Fleur's naked body slide down his. Her tongue made him groan.

Monty threw his head back and closed his eyes. He moaned again. "Whew yes Fleur, that's the spot. Damn, I love performing charity for a worthy cause," he murmured with delight. "Yes…Yes I do!"

Chapter 18

Misunderstanding & other riddles...

Across the crowded dance floor Louis strode coolly and confidently toward the main ballroom. It was setup theater-style for the pageant performance.He quickly pushed aside the heavy velvet curtains that were set up to cover the stage.

"Hey, Clare Palling, where is Mother Kahina Laveau? We need to get this pageant underway," he confidently said.

Clare Palling was an accountant by trade. She was here to make sure all receipts and expenses were accounted for at the charity event.

"The last time I saw her she was with her daughter Noita."

"Noita?" he repeated, with a puzzled expression.

"You know Noita. She is the one everyone calls Miss Mary Mackeey. They were trying to calm some girl's parents."

Clare fussed with a couple of folders. "You know, I don't know how Mother Laveau can do it, dealing with those fickle teenage girls in the Royal Queen Pageant. I would much rather deal with the kids in the Junior Royal Court any day," she said nodding. "Their parents don't feel they are owed a thing."

The Royal Queen Pageant was not the only highlight of the Grand Isles Christmas Ball. Young ladies aged fifteen to twenty competed to be crowned the Royal Queen of the Grand Isles Christmas Ball. The pageant brought in a huge chunk of the donations.

The Junior Royal Court was the children's pageant. Children from grades third all the way up to sixth grade were selected for the title of King, Queen, Prince, Princess, Duke, Duchess, Count and Countess based upon their community and academic achievements.

Louis rubbed his face. "What happened now?"

Clare breathed out. "Oh, you know how it always goes. Some parents think they can buy their way to the Royal Queen Pageant. It seems one of the girls feels she's being slighted. So, she yelled for her mommy and daddy. Her hyper-emotional parents came backstage to yell their disbelief that they haven't donated enough money for their daughter to win."

Louis shook his head. "What?"

"You know the old story Louis. The parents only donated money hoping it would guarantee their daughter was going to win the pageant tonight," she said smothering a yarn. "I think Mother Kahina Laveau has it all under control. Anyway, they took their argument out back into the corridor heading toward the kitchen. Come on, I'll take you to them."

Louis fell in alongside Clare Palling. She led him through the back door into the hallway.

Mother Kahina Laveau looked up. "Ah Louis, I'm so glad you're here. I believe your help is needed."

Clare nudged Louis. "I'll leave you to handle this," she said turning and leaving the way she came.

Louis watched as the door closed behind her. Clare didn't want to deal with this situation. He didn't blame her. Slowly he turned and looked up. "What can I help you with Mother Laveau?"

"I believe this young lady and her family would like to have her name scratched as one of the entries for the queen pageant tonight," she said with a pause, turning to the young woman. "Isn't that what you and your parents would like Katrina?"

"No! Katrina shook her head. "There just seems to be a misunderstanding."

The atmosphere in the small office was chaotic.

Only Mother Kahina Laveau seemed unfazed by the drama.

The Baptiste family was known for their large real estate holdings. Jean Baptiste owned a large real estate company. His family could trace their roots back to the Spanish land grants of 1855.

Jean Baptiste cleared his throat. "Yes, that is exactly what we would like. I want to pull our daughter from the competition and ask for a full return of our donated monies, and my wife Pauline agrees with me."

Katrina Baptiste looked up at her father. "Daddy, are you crazy? I may as well become suicidal and kill myself tonight."

"Stop being over dramatic Katrina," her father said.

"Mother tell father. If he asks for the money back, people will be talking about this for years to come," she said with a determined tilt of her chin. "I will not pull out of tonight's competition."

Pauline Baptiste stood silently while taking in the situation. She could tell by her daughter's cold stares that she wanted her to intervene. Pauline had learned how to tell what Katrina's various stares meant.

She stood for a moment and held Katrina's gaze unflinching. She figured that, maybe, if she stood her ground and didn't give into her, something could change.

Then Katrina's eyes flashed cold back at her. It was the stare she dreaded.If she didn't side with her daughter, she would dread it.

Pauline Baptiste's eyes narrowed into slants as she stared back at her husband. "Katrina's right Jean," she said. "You will make this family the butt of everyone's jokes, if you ask for our money back."

Their one daughter Katrina Baptiste had fine-elegant bone structure and a great figure like her mother. But she was taller with the advantages of youth and beauty.Being the only daughter, she had learned long ago how to get her father to do her bidding. "Daddy, please don't pull me out of tonight's competition," her voice pleaded.

Jean Baptiste rolled his eyes. "Look Katrina, go find Clare Palling, and see if there is anything, she needs for you to do," he said waiving his hand.

"Fine, I'm out of here," Katrina shouted, doing as she was told and slamming the exit door behind her.

Jean turned and faced Louis. "All right Louis. I understand your view without being told. But my wife, well now she needs to hear the words. So, make this clear," he said rubbing his brow. "Am I to understand the amount of money I donated here tonight will not make any difference in my daughter being crowned queen?"

"For once Jean we are on the same page," Louis said remaining calm.

Jean Baptiste turned to his wife. "Do you hear the man dear? He can't make it any clearer than that."

"Jean, you don't think I'm a simpleton, do you? I heard the man loud and clear," Pauline said.

Jean paced as if deep in thought.

Pauline glanced up at Louis. She hesitated for a slight moment. "Louis, I thought this year the Queen Pageant was going to be rated by which girl brought in the most money."

Louis raised his brow. "No Pauline, this issue was voted down at the event planning meeting. You remember? You raised it."

Pauline shrugged and waived her hand "As I recall, the vote wasn't final on the issue."

Louis shrugged. "If you don't believe me ask Nate Trent. He's the committee chairperson and he is one of the pageant judges."

Pauline stared back a t Louis with a frown marring her brow. "Yes…Yes…Yes he is. I'd forgotten."

Suddenly Jean Baptiste abruptly stopped pacing. He had a thought. He turned and stared at his wife with wide eyes. "Damn Pauline, I hope this isn't some kind of mess you're cooking up in that scheming mind of yours. Look, I thought you and I agreed to pull Katrina out of the competition, if it wasn't going to be judged by who raised the most money, period."

Pauline reached down and opened her purse. She pulled out her compact and checked her makeup. "I agreed to do what makes Katrina happy. Not bringing disgrace to our family by asking for our donation back."

Jean shook his head. "But what if Katrina loses? Have you thought of that Pauline?"

"Oh Jean, how can you say such a thing?" Pauline asked.

Nervously Jean stuffed his hands into his pockets. "This is crazy Pauline. Let's just take our money and our daughter and just go home."

Mother Kahina Laveau was a skilled negotiator. She tilted her head coquettishly. "Jean, if you cannot afford to make a donation to this worthy cause, perhaps you should ask for your money back. If you can't afford it, you can't afford it," she said flashing him a big smile.

Jean clenched his hand into a fist. "The Baptiste family is not destitute!"

Pauline whirled around. "Now see what you've done Jean. You've got people thinking we're poor. Not to mention, we do not want to anger Mother Laveau or her daughter Miss Mackey, the famous clairvoyant."

Jean Baptiste frowned. "Fine, I'm going home Pauline. I don't want any parts of this," he said abruptly turning to leave.

Pauline watched her husband slam the door behind him. She turned and stared between Mother Kahina Laveau and Louis. She opened her mouth closed it and then gave them a look of commiseration. "Oh, never mind," she said somberly turning to leave.

Mother Kahina Laveau hooked her finger and signaled Louis to come over.

Louis strolled over and stood next to Mother Kahina Laveau. She leaned in close and whispered.

"Well, Louis, let the games begin."

Chapter 19

Sparkling Eyes...

Rogmar Womack thought Celica Baptiste was the most beautiful woman he'd ever met. The romantic garden room was the perfect place to slow dance.

Rog smiled softly. "I should let you have a rest. I've been dancing with you for almost an hour," he said. "I'm sure you must be tired of me by now."

Celica smiled back at him ruefully. "I was hoping to dance with you for another hour. I'm having a good time."

Rog gave her an envious look. "But what about your friends? Especially that tall fellow I saw you with earlier. He must be wondering what's happened to you."

Celica giggled and let Rog take her arm. They walked a few steps. "Is that your way of telling me your feet hurt? Anyway, don't look so jealous. That was just my employer you saw me with earlier."

A moment later, they took a seat.

"You're staring at me again Rog."

Rog grinned wide, staring back at her. "You know, you're beautiful. I mean really beautiful. Did you know that your eyes sparkle like diamonds? At first, I thought it was just the romantic lighting in here.

But now I'm sure it your eyes."

A shiver ran down her spine. She felt like she had waited for Rog all her life.

They sat in silence.

Finally, Rog broke the ice. "Celica, I'm so glad you suggested we come and dance in the garden. It is so romantic here."

"And thank you for agreeing to come and dance with me. I feel like I've known you forever," she said, staring at his chest.

The gold buttons on his uniform shined in the romantic light. She wondered what he looked like with his jacket off. Celica stared again at his chest.She caught him looking. "Ah, I was just thinking, I'm so thirsty."

"Would you like for me to get you a drink?"

"No, I would like for you to kiss me," Celica smiled.

"I was hoping you asked. He leaned over and softly kissed her lips.

She inhaled his aftershave. She knew the brand. It was as American as American could be. It was Old Spice. It smelled wonderful on him. She shivered from the goose bumps it gave her.

The kiss was light. Then the kiss erupted hard and passionate.

Abruptly Celica pulled away. "Oh! I just had an idea."

Her eyes sparkled brightly.

Rog began hesitantly. "You are doing that sparkle thing again with your eyes," he smiled softly. "What is it? Do you want me to go and get some good seats so that we can see the Royal Pageant together, huh?"

Celica looked directly at him and said, "No. I was thinking that maybe you'd like to go up to my room and have a drink…But," she said as her voice trailed off thinking it had been a bad idea.

"Why Miss Celica, you intend to ask me up to your room, have your way with me and then run off and leave me, don't you?"

Celica hung her head feeling rejected.

Rog laughed and then pushed back a strand of her hair lightly. "Don't worry Celica. I've wanted to sleep with you from the moment I saw you too, if that's any conciliation."

Her eyes challenged his. "Rog, just so you know, I'm not a shy little flower and I'm not a damaged human being. But I do like sex."

Rog reached out a large hand. He touched the side of her face gently and then let his hand trace down and cupped her breast. His voice was barely a whisper. "And I love having sex in as many positions as possible. And don't worry I have a pocket full of condoms."

Celica giggled and took his hand in hers. She pulled him along toward the elevators.

Chapter 20

Smug arrogance...

After that disastrous meeting with Jean and Louis, Pauline left the office and started to walk. She walked down the long corridor past the bar.

She looked into the bar but didn't see anyone she knew. She didn't see Ming Mondragon and that was who she'd hoped to find.

She continued walking to the back of the hotel past the coffee shop. The area was deserted. The quietness helped clear her thoughts.

Suddenly she heard footsteps behind her.

"Mother, I thought that was you. Well, what happened in there? Is daddy asking for his money back?"

Startled, Pauline almost jumped out of her skin. Where did you come from Katrina?" she asked but didn't wait for a response. "You're still in the pageant. I'm sure that is what you really wanted to ask about."

Katrina diverted her eyes. "I...I was talking with Jorge when I saw you walk past."

Pauline flashed a knowing smile. She'd look in the bar before she walked past hoping to spot Ming. "Come again Katrina."

Katrina felt a trickle of alarm at her mother's stare. "Okay Mother,

I saw you when you walked past the bar. I was sitting in the back, behind the plant trellis."

Pauline nodded. "Just as I thought," she said. "I thought I saw you sitting back in the corner. Have you seen Ming Mondragon? I can't seem to find her anywhere."

Katrina bit her lip. "No mother, I haven't seen Ming. Now can we focus on me here? Tell me what happened. Will I be crowned Queen of the Royal Queen Pageant tonight based on Daddy's donation?"

"No," Pauline regarded her with concern. "You have to earn the title. The judges will decide who is crowned Queen."

"Judges? What judges?"

Pauline waved her hand. "Oh you know. The same ones that sit on the panel every year. Nate Trent and a couple others," she hesitated.

Katrina's thoughts raced. Being crowned Queen was too important to leave it up to chance. She stared back at her mother. The only things she thought were important were her expensively dyed bleached blond hair and keeping her great figure in va-va-voom condition. She didn't understand her need to win the queen title.

Katrina clenched her fist by her side as she stood there trying to think of what to do. For a long time, she'd felt her mother was just jealous of her. Now that she had stood and watched mother standing idling by not taking her being crowned this year's queen seriously, she knew it was true. The thought made her angry. She'd show her this time. She would take control. This time would be different. She felt rage. She clenched her fist tighter.

Reluctantly Katrina shook her head and took a step back. Not sure why. The last thing she'd ever do was hit her mother. Her father Jean would have a fit if she did. She knew her father loved her mother strongly. Her thoughts churned. There was still time. The main Royal pageant wouldn't take place for at least a couple of hours. There was still hope for her. She would make sure that crown was hers.

"Who holds the official judge title mother? Who has the position of power?"

"Position of power," Pauline laughed out. "Position of power my ass. I'm not sure if there is such a thing. The only thing I ever thought Nate was good for was standing by grinning like an idiot. But he is the official judge. His vote decides the winner."

Katrina laughed back nervously. She didn't want her mother to suspect a thing. "But Dad has way more power than Nate will ever have, right?"

Pauline thought she detected something in her daughter's voice. She studied her face and thought she detected a trace of smug arrogance. She hoped Katrina wasn't thinking of doing anything stupid. She prayed her daughter wasn't that stupid. Maybe it was her imagination. She took her daughters hand. "Yes, you know that's true," she shrugged. "But I guess Nate is probably second in power to your father and first in power on the pageant committee," she took a deep breath. "My goodness Katrina you made me laugh so hard it made me thirsty. Come on, let's go and have a glass of punch."

Katrina hesitated deep in her thoughts.

"Baby girl, a penny for your thoughts, winning isn't everything they claim it to be," Pauline said with a hint of caution in her voice.

Katrina stole a peek at her mother. "Gosh Mom," she yawned, hiding her true feelings. "I'm feeling so harried. I think I'll go up to my room and relax before the Royal Queen Pageant starts."

"Darling, you do look a little tired. You go on up and I'll come up and check on you."

"Oh no Mother," Katrina nervously exclaimed. "I need you to go and make sure my cheering squad is in order."

Hesitantly, Pearl took a step back. "Yeah, sure baby, mommy can do that. I'll make sure I have your cheering squad all in order," her eyes searched hers. "If that's what you really want me to do."

Katrina reached out and hugged her mother briefly. Her expression hid her true motives. "Yes mother, that's what I want. I need you to make sure Ming and the girls are all there as my cheering squad. Go and find seats for everyone or something," she said dismissing her, as she abruptly walked away.

Chapter 21

The Womanizer, Blame it on alcohol...

Minutes later Pauline settled into a chair at the bar. With one hand she clasped her glass and then brought the straw to her lips. The drink felt good going down.

She stared back at the ceiling to floor mirror in front of her. It reflected back the corridor leading to the main hallway back toward the front of the hotel.

It didn't take long for Pauline to focus her eyes on the two men standing under a huge elaborate Spanish Revivalist painting on the wall.

She glanced back intently. They wore uniforms with gold buttons and black arm slashes. She looked again and saw the letters MP on their arms.

Then a thought struck her. She wondered if they were looking for one of the young men present at the event.

Pauline hadn't turned the thought over in her mind when she heard someone call her name.

"Pauline?" a woman's delicate voice asked, taking the seat next to her.

"Pearl, what are you doing here?"

"I just needed a moment to myself," Pearl shrugged her shoulders taking a seat beside her. "I was backstage with Mother Kahina Laveau, but the loud chatter of children trying to talk over each other was getting on my nerves. How Mother Laveau can stand it I'll never know. And you?"

"My nerves were on edge too. But for different reasons."

Pearl's eyes grew thoughtful. "Say, what's that you're drinking? It looks mighty thirst quenching."

"It is," Pauline swallowed hard and waived her hand. "Darn, I forgot what it is called," she took the final sip, swallowed hard and then put the empty glass back on the counter.

Pauline then paused a moment. She rubbed her brow as if she was trying to remember.

"Say Bartender, my friend Pearl will have one of these," she said lifting her drink. "What's it called again?" she asked but didn't wait for him to answer. "Oh, never mind, and bring me another one too."

Minutes later, the bartender walked over with their drinks.

"Bartender, what's this drink called again," Pauline asked as he placed her drink in front of her.

"Madam, the drink is called a Sloe Gin Fizz," the bartender said.

"Well, ain't that a cute name," Pauline smiled.

She nodded and lifted her glass up and Pearl took the hint.

Pauline and Pearl clinked glasses together.

Pearl took a sip from her straw. "Gosh this is good, thanks for suggesting it."

"No problem," Pauline nodded.

"Say Pauline, do you have some sort of man trouble?" Pearl curiously asked.

"Not exactly. My trouble is called daughter trouble. And she thinks mommy is stupid."

"Oh?"

"Yeah, you see my daughter wants to be Queen, but she doesn't understand. Mommy and Daddy can't buy her everything."

Pearl nodded her head in understanding.

All at once Pauline raised her brow. "What about you Pearl? Do you have man trouble?" she gently asked.

Pearl nodded her head. "No…No… I'm afraid not," she lied hoping Pauline didn't notice.

"That's too bad. Man trouble is the most sinful and sensually stimulating trouble to have," she said raising a mock toast.

Pearl took a big swig on her straw. Before she could answer, a man emerged in the doorway of the bar. Her eyes glanced up toward the tall man as recognition hit.

"Don't look now Pauline, but I believe you've just summoned up yourself some stimulating man trouble. There's your husband Jean Baptiste," Pearl said with a nod.

"Huh?" Pauline turned around in her seat. She smiled softly, slanting her eyes to focus.

Her eyes beheld Jean Baptiste staring back at her lovingly.

"Pauline, please come dance with me," Jean Baptiste's deep voice tenderly sliced the air. "There's a romantic garden area on the second floor and it made me think of you."

"I thought you left Jean. I'm so glad you didn't," she murmured, smiling wide. "Oh yes, I will come and dance with you. Yes, I will!" Pauline repeated, as she rushed over making her way to him.

Pearl watched Pauline and Jean Baptiste leaving arm in arm. "Damn that lucky bitch, Jean loves her very much," she murmured under her breath.

"Envious are we Pearl? I can see Louis leaving you alone all the time is starting to take a toll?"

Pearl clenched her teeth. "Monty! Where did you come from? You really shouldn't eavesdrop on other people's conversations."

"For your information I wasn't eavesdropping. I was sitting beside the two of you unnoticed, the whole time," he said, finishing off his drink and waiving for the bartender.

Silence fell.

The bartender rushed over and quickly gave him a fresh drink.

Monty picked up his glass and sipped. Finally, he broke the ice. His grin was easy like a triumphant man who'd just won a god medal. "Let me tell you about yourself Pearl. You married young. Too young," he paused. "Before you had a chance to experience life," his gaze held hers. It promised everything. "You're a woman that needs to be loved. You're starved for it. I won't be a fake liar with you, Pearl. I want to go to bed with you, not only because I know I've fallen madly in love with you, but because your body is starving for attention. It's calling out to me," he licked his lips. "I bet you've never slept with anyone but your husband Louis, have you?"

Pearl's eyes narrowed. She hadn't expected his directness. "You've got some nerve Monty."

Monty touched her arm as he looked into her eyes. "Why, because I believe every woman has the right, in her life-time, to experience the best hot wicked sex she's ever had," he paused to let his words set in.

His fingers slowly caressed her hand and slowly edged up her arm. "You know the kind. The kind that can fulfill and satisfy that deep sexual hunger a woman has all pent up inside of her. The kind she can remember for a lifetime."

They glanced between each other.

Pearl realized Monty was loaded with a lot of hot and spicy words and some of it was the most exceptionally sweet talk she'd ever heard. Grudgingly Pearl tried to look away. She had to admit that Monty had her number down. Tonight, was the first night in months that Louis had spent any time with her. The dance they'd shared together had not been enough. Knowing Louis, he had probably penciled her into his night's agenda.

Pearl sighed, thinking how she'd been patient every year for the months leading up to the Grand Isle Ball. Every year it was the same. Louis would be too busy to notice her. A few nights before she'd dress in a black lace veiled negligee' and climb into bed beside Louis, only to find he had fallen fast asleep. As usual he'd be too busy to show his wife any affection or give her the much-needed attention she craved. Her body felt starved.

Monty lost himself in Pearl's beautiful face. He could tell she was tormented by her thoughts. He studied her while her mind was distracted. She was just where he wanted her to be.

She was the kind of woman a man wanted to give everything he owned to. He reached out and clasped her hand in his. Her skin felt so soft.

Pearl looked up into Monty's eyes. His eyes flickered wickedly back at her with hot desire. He wanted her.

"It's getting hot in here," she said swallowing hard. "I…I need to get going Monty."

His eyes looked at her tenderly. His voice was soft. "I've never wanted anyone the way I want you Pearl. I swear. I'm sorry if I offended you. But I had to get that off of my chest. It's hard to find a good woman like you Pearl. I envy Louis. Forgive me," he reached out and took her hand and brought it to his lips. "If I ever got the chance, I could love you better. I could satisfy you."

Pearl felt weak. Her resolve was dissolving.

"Have a drink with me. As a friend," his eyes pleaded. "Please?"

"Sure," Pearl said with a nod. She couldn't seem to say no to him. She lifted her glass.

"Here's to a woman of few words and great beauty. Mrs. Pearl La Cour, a woman full of all the right stuff," he said swallowing his drink.

Pearl quietly watched Monty. For some reason she couldn't seem to raise the glass to her lips.

"Drink up Pearl, drink up," Monty said encouragingly. He kept his eyes on her drink. Watching her bring it to her lips.

All at once Pearl turned her head. She caught a glimpse of something.

The atmosphere in the room seemed to change suddenly.

"What a strange feeling," she said bewildered.

The room enfolded like a serene heavy fog. It carried a feeling as if something not of this world.

"What is it Pearl?"

"Can you feel it? It reminds me of something. Something my grandmother would call having a visit. You know someone visiting from out of the past," she shivered. "Don't you feel it Monty?"

Silence hung in the air at that moment as slowly a woman's body came into view in front of her. She had curly kinky red hair and large saucer-wide innocent blue eyes.

Pearl shook her head she was speechless. At that moment she was thankful her grandmother, Madeleine Chaminade, had been born with second sight. She had taught her many things and told her that there were a lot of things that didn't belong to this world.

The woman was like a dream, a ethereal creature of peace come to life. She wasn't ordinary. She reached out and took Pearl's drink. Her silvery and emotionless voice penetrated the air. "I'll toast with him, if you like."

Monty shook his head and looked back at the redheaded woman. "Baby, where have you been all of my life?" he asked curiously, as if held in a trance.

Pearl looked up at the woman and forced herself to consider the possibility that she was hallucinating. The more she stared at the ethereal redheaded woman, the more she knew that there was an angel underneath that mop of red hair. She supposed that a sinner like Monty didn't stand a chance. Everyone knew Angels preferred Geeks to sinners.

Pearl gave a short laugh. She wasn't amused. "Well, Monty. I guess that's my signal to leave. I'll be seeing you. Oh, and enjoy your new friend. If she stays around you long enough," she whispered under her breath with a deep knowing as she headed for the exit.

"Bye Pearl," Monty said eying the redheaded woman as if he'd been in love with her forever.

Seconds later Monty shook his head. He felt strange. "Pearl…Pearl. Hey wait a minute. I don't know what I'm doing. I swear it. It must be the alcohol. Come back Pearl," he called after her. Quickly he turned around. "Say lady what did you put in my drink?" he rubbed his brow. "Did you switch our drinks?"

The red headed lady laughed.

Chapter 22

I've got a plan...

Katrina figured if she shut her eyes and concentrated hard enough, she could believe the hands that were cupping her breasts were Jorge Manteau's. The thought of being naked in bed with Nate Trent made Katrina nauseated. But he was on the board of directors at one of Silicon Valley's oldest Foundations and he was the head judge on the pageant board.

Nate Trent stared back at the naked young woman in front of him as if he was hypnotized. She was the younger beautiful spitting image of her mother except for the blond hair.

He thought back into his memories. He licked his lips. He'd always wanted to screw Pauline Baptiste. He'd even spent time trying to be her best friend. He remembered when Jean's business kept him too occupied to take time with his wife. Pauline had been lonely and friendless. She had attended the Foundations committee meeting religiously. But the other women on the committee had been jealous of her. None of them would befriend her.

Nate had made it a point to be her friend. He had taken the time to make Pauline feel special, even taking her out to dinner after their weekly committee meetings and going shoe shopping with her. He missed no opportunity to get close to her. But she'd never let him have anything to do with her sexually. She looked down her nose at him when he'd asked her point blank why she wouldn't sleep with him. She told him she loved her husband Jean Baptiste too much to ever cheat on him.

Her words had stung like the venomous bite of a poisonous snake when Pauline told him that. But that was years ago. Now he didn't care. He could pretend her daughter was her.

Nate gently set his lips on Katrina's, tasting her, savoring her.

Katrina murmured out a groan. "You promise me Nate?"

Sweat ran down Nate's face. The girl had reached out and touched his penis. He shuddered from the feeling it gave.

"Yeah honey, I promise. You make sure I enjoy screwing you and I swear that crown is yours," he grunted. "I'm the power behind that pageant's panel. I make all the decisions," he said running his hands up and down her body.

Katrina shimmered in closer and let her hand cup his behind. She squeezed. "You ride me hard now Nate and I'll give you the best ride of your life."

"Just hold on tight sweetie! Just hold on tight," he grinned.

Katrina shut her eyes tighter and thrilled at the glorious surge of power. She had a plan and Nate Trent would help her put it into action.

All at once Katrina started uttering moans of incredulous ecstasy that she was sure to arouse Nate's sensual pleasure.

"Oh, Nate you are so amazing," she moaned.

"Yes…Yes…I am," Nate said grinning wide.

Chapter 23

Memories don't leave like people do...

Pearl walked as quickly and quietly as she dared down the silent dark corridor. Finally, dim lighting above a glass door greeted her. The words written on the glass door said Pool.

Her hand gripped the door handle firmly. It gave as she pushed. The roof top pool area was open.

She closed the door behind her and stopped abruptly. She let her eyes skim the roof-top pool area. She didn't spot him. The bright lights illuminating from the pool made the water look mystic blue. She listened attentively. She was alone.

She sighed. She could have sworn she saw him enter.

The night sky made the area feel strange and lonely.

She thought she heard a sound behind her.

All at once a man's deep voice sliced the air.

"Why are you following me little girl?"

Pearl whirled around instinctively. Her eyes looked in the direction of the voice. She smiled wide.

"Horace," she said smiling as something stirred in her heart.

Horace Sherlock Garrison's silhouette emerged from the darkness. He walked slowly into the light.

"My goodness Horace, you scared me!" She breathed out.

"Pearl, I intended to," Horace's voice was cold and stern as he stepped closer. He swallowed hard. "What are you doing here? You're a married woman. You shouldn't be sneaking around in the dark, alone."

His harsh words weren't what she came for. They made her feel so alone in the world. Pearl hung her head and walked slowly over to the side of the pool. She stood for a moment with her thoughts, before tilting her head and looking up at the night sky.

Horace slowly joined her. "That sure is a beautiful sky out tonight," he said pausing and staring above into the sky.

Overhead the steel blue of night sky was brightly lit with stars.

Pearl sighed heavily. As they both stood there studying the night sky. She tilted her head and looked him over. He looked so handsome. "I've been looking for you Horace. I saw you when you first came in. I didn't get a chance to say hello."

Horace didn't say anything for a moment. As he thought, Louis La Cour was a lucky man. He had a family he could be proud of. A robust intelligent son, a lovely daughter and a beautiful wife that was standing in front of him. He'd bet money Louis wouldn't give them up for all the money in the world.

He took a deep breath and let it out. "I know I saw you with your daughter, Lacey," he nodded. "By the way, she looks just like you. You always did want a little girl," he said, as his eyes searched her face.

She thought she heard the anguish in his voice. She glanced around making sure they were alone. "I needed to talk to you Horace," her eyes pleaded. "You and I are old childhood friends. We are both from the same place."

Horace gave her a sympathetic smile. "Oh, now I know what this is about, Pearl," he shook his head. "I should have known. You're homesick again. It's the month of December. You always get melancholy in December. Remember? That's because your Grandmere Madeleine died on Christmas day. This month has always made you sad."

"No…No…I'm lonely. Very lonely," she choked out. "I can feel it in my bones Horace. I can feel it in my bones," she repeated and stared straight ahead.

He frowned with a heavy sigh. "I'll suggest to Louis that he should send for some of your kin folks to come out and visit you. You'll get over your loneliness real fast then. Better yet, maybe I should just tell Louis to take you back home to Louisiana for a visit."

Pearl closed her eyes. She shook her head. "No…No… You do not understand me, Horace," her voice pleaded. "I'm living with memories of decisions I've made. Every day I struggle with them and I'm miserable behind them."

"What decisions?" Horace asked emphatically.

"My marriage to Louis for one thing," Pearl said. "There are problems with my marriage. First off I was just a kid when I married Louis."

"That's the past Pearl. Let it go. We all made stupid decisions when we were kids," Horace said. "Just let it go. Now you're acting like a spoiled child. You are not a child anymore Pearl. You are an adult and a mother first."

"What is that supposed to mean Horace? You're treating me like a child now."

"That's because you're acting like one. You're not looking at your priorities right now. You don't see the big picture," he ruminated. "You are a mother and your children should always come first."

Suddenly tears formed in Pearl's eyes. It had been useless trying to talk to Horace alone. He didn't understand. Maybe he never did.

Pearl gave a silent shaking shrug. Tears begin streaming down her face. "You bastard! You're the one acting like a child. Horace, you are acting like an asshole.I don't know why I even tried to talk to you."

He heard the cry in her voice as she drew in a sharp inhale.

Horace winced. "Wait a minute Pearl. Calm down. You've never spoken to me like this before. I'm your best friend. We grew up together. You're my family."

"Go fuck yourself Horace!" she hissed, with a disgusted tone in her voice. "And don't you follow me!" Pearl yelled as she ran from the room. She slammed the door behind her with a bang.

Horace stood silently for a few minutes and ran his fingers through his hair. It was obvious he didn't want to be seen leaving too soon after Pearl. Finally, he straightened his jacket and strode across to the door and slammed it behind him.

A short distance away, in the darkened solitude, a man watched the scene play out silently, in the dark. Jealousy tormented him as he moved slowly into the light. His face was contorted with agony. The miserable stupid little whore was just like any other woman. Behind his eyes, he felt a buildup of pain. He should have never followed her. He passed a hand over the throbbing pain behind his eyes. He touched his eyes. They felt wet. He was crying. The corners of his lips twitched. "Well I'll be damned," the man muttered under his breath.

Chapter 24

An Embarrassing Situation...

Rog laid comfortable in the bed. "Darling you are not a shy thing! I love it that you are so active in the bedroom and you're beautiful, you're superb," Rog whispered as his hand molded around her breast.

The man is a handsome and thoughtful sexy machine! Celica thought as she stared back at him remembering how her body felt when Rog had brought her to her last climax.

At first, when she saw Rog standing naked before her, she had felt as jittery as when he'd first asked her to dance. She'd made him wait while she downed a couple more glasses of champagne before she felt lightheaded enough to jump on him, straddling him, as she pinned him to the bed.

Their lovemaking had been fierce and passionate. She hadn't felt that much pleasure with a man in a long time.

Rog rose up and got out of bed. He reached for the bottle of champagne and poured. He handed her a drink.

"Here's to the Celica Baptiste –You're everything a man could want."

They clinked glasses.

"Let's order some dinner," Celica suggested.

"Isn't it about time we returned to the ballroom? I thought you needed to be there when the Queen is crowned?"

"Things have changed. I'm having a great time," she said. "Besides, I'd much rather have room service with you. Aren't you hungry?"

Rog leaned over. "Of course," he said softly brushing her lips with a kiss.

"Good, that settles that. Do you like pasta?" she asked without waiting for an answer. "They have the best Chicken Primavera here."

"Great, I'll have extra chicken on mine."

Celica reached for the phone.

Twenty minutes later. Rog laid stroking Celica's shoulders as they lay in bed together.

There was a knock at the door.

"Gosh that was quick," Rog said. "I haven't even had time to put my boxers back on," he said reaching for his underpants.

"Good, because I am famished," she reached and pulled the sheet tighter around her."Just have room service add the check to my suite."

Rog walked to the door and opened it. Instantly recognition hit.

"Almighty God! Oh, shit!" Rog loudly screamed.

Several men entered the room.

Celica flamed in fury. "How dare you come in here? This is a private room. Get out! Get out!"

The men ignored her and tussled Rog to the floor.

"Rog…Rog! Who are these men? Let him go…Let him go!" She shrieked loudly, clinging to the sheet.

Rog lay handcuffed on the floor. He stopped struggling. "Celica they're fucking MPs. Oh shit! Oh shit! The handcuff is too tight."

One of the MPs knelt over Rog on the floor. "Okay soldier get dressed. Put your pants on or I'll put them on for you."

Another MP turned and focused his attention on Celica as she lay in the bed. "Lady this man is under military arrest."

"Military arrest," she repeated, puzzled. What for?"

"Lady that's classified information," the MP said.

Dressed, the MPs headed Rog toward the door. Abruptly he stopped.

"Sir, can I just say something to the lady?"

The MPs nodded.

Rog turned and looked back at Celica. His eyes were sorrowful. "Being here with you this past couple of hours and getting to know you Celica, I feel I've got, to be honest with you. I'm afraid I haven't been a truthful man with you."

Celica looked puzzled. "Rog what is it?"

Rog shrugged his shoulders. "I'm not talking about my being arrested by the military police. That's classified like the MP said," the corner of his lip twitched. "I'm talking about my being married."

"Married!"

"Yes," Rog said. "I just wanted to tell you so that you didn't run out and try and help me or something like that. Your good people Celica," he paused. "But you see my wife wouldn't understand. Nor would she like it very much if you showed up at the military hearing or anything."

Aghast Celica stared back dumbfounded. She felt so humiliated. A married looser she thought. She could really pick them.

Rog felt relieved telling her the truth. It was a load off of his mind. He shook his head. Now was the moment of truth.

"Oh yeah Celica, there's one more thing. Tell Monty I would have slept with you for free. You deserve more than being the object of some guy's stupid joke. Anyway, too bad I didn't get a chance to really take you out and give you the full Rog treatment. You know, wining and dining you like I was paid to," he shrugged. "I would have really loved to get to know you better."

Celica's mouth dropped open as if she'd been hit by a bolt of lightning. "I don't believe it. You're lying."

"Sorry Celica, but it's true. Monty paid me to pick you up tonight. I was supposed to see you for a couple of weeks before I broke things off with you. That was the deal with Monty. But considering I'm being arrested, there has to be a change in plans," he said with a sly grin.

Celica breathed out. The moment was awkward.

Rog shrugged. "You know, now that I think about it. This thing with my being arrested, it all reeks of one of Monty's games," he said dryly. "I beat he called the MPs and told them I was here tonight with you. Good thing I made him pay me in advance."

Instantly, she knew Rog was telling the truth. She'd seen Monty use people and play games with them before. But he'd never subjected her to one of his games. She was furious.

Celica looked back at Rog with a distressed expression for a long moment before she cleared her throat and said.

"Hey, you MPs, please get him out of my room."

Chapter 25

For old times' sake show some love ...

Pearl ran down the corridor and took the elevator. She rode it down several floors and then pushed the button and got off. I can't believe the nerve of that man!"

"Is there something wrong Pearl?"

"Christ!" She jumped and turned to stare. There towering above her was Monty Wildhorse.

"Monty, what are you doing here?"

"Taking the elevator."

Pearl tried to avert her eyes. Her emotions from the episode earlier with Horace Garrison were fresh. She fought the rush of tears, aware now that her friendship as well as her love for Horace were well out of her grasp. "This is my floor, Monty," she sobbed out feeling the crush of the weight of her lost love and friendship with Horace.

"I was just on my way down to the main ballroom," he hesitated, noticing her make-up was smeared. "But I'm willing to postpone it. You look like you could use a friend Pearl."

Pearl felt helpless and friendless. She let her hand touch her face. She didn't want anyone to see her like this.

She tried to smile. "Oh...I... I'd hate for anyone to see me like this."

"Come Pearl," he said reaching for her hand. "Let's clean you up and have a drink together. It will clear your thoughts. You need a friend. Let me be your friend."

Gently Monty's fingers took her hand. His touch was warm. Slowly his hand clasped over hers. He didn't want to frighten her. She looked like a deer caught in headlights.

Pearl felt like she was in a fog.

Monty pulled her into an embrace. "I love you Pearl. Can't you see I've done everything I can to be with you tonight?" his head moved in to kiss her.

Enthusiastically Monty kissed her.

"Get your hands off of my wife Monty," Louis' voice coldly ripped the air.

A fit of jealous rage consumed Monty as he spun around. Instantly he released Pearl from his embraced.

"Louis!" Pearl exclaimed, trying to tear her eyes away from the pain she saw in his eyes.

Louis was only a step away from them.

"Damn, I'm getting a little tired of you men thinking my wife is up for grabs. I protect mine, and I don't appreciate men I thought were my friends trying to pick up my lady."

She stepped away. "Louis I… was just so confused. I'm so sorry…"

"Shhhhh. Pearl," Louis said softly. He caringly stared back at Pearl. His eyes told her he knew she wasn't romantically interested in Monty.

Quickly he closed the distance between them and got in Monty's face. "Right now, Monty, all I feel like doing is kicking that flea ridden arse of yours for kissing my wife. But doing so would only keep me from telling my wife how much I love her and how much I know I've been neglecting her and how much I wish I could do the thing I want to do most," Louis hesitated. "And that is taking my wife back to our suite and making love to her."

A knot of cold-hearted jealousy took hold of Monty deep in his gut at the sound of Louis' words. He'd had his heart set on making love to Pearl tonight. Louis had cheated him. No one cheated Monty out of anything. With a laugh, Monty shook his head. At that moment he hated Louis. Pretending to not notice him he let his hand swing out toward Louis.

"Louis, watch out," Pearl screamed.

Louis anticipated his move. He ducked and landed a punch so powerful to the side of Monty's face. He crumpled to the floor.

The moment was tense.

Monty cupped his jaw in agony. "You can have that bitch, Louis," he viciously croaked out.

Louis took a step toward him poised to attack. "Don't insult my wife!"

"Louis don't. Monty looks hurt," Pearl said as she cautiously put her hand on Louis' shoulder.

Monty threw his hand up surrendering.

"Hold on a minute Louis. I'm sorry about that little remark," he said swaying a little trying to stand. "Damn, I didn't think you were willing to fight for your wife's honor."

Monty checked his teeth making sure they were all there. Louis had hit him hard. He leaned against the wall to steady himself. He hated the way Pearl had looked at him when he fell. Now he hated the tender way she was looking at Louis.He wiped his mouth. He'd make her pay."Oh, and Louis, if I were you I'd ask Pearl why she keeps running behind your back trying to see that guy Horace Garrison," he shrugged. "Personally, I don't think Pearl wants either one of us."

Aghast, Pearl sucked in a deep breath.

Monty smiled indignantly. By the look of the expression on Pearl's face, she knew she was in trouble with Louis.

He gave her a wicked sinister smile. "Good night Pearl. I hope you have to do a hell of a lot of explaining to convenience Louis you weren't cheating on him with Horace," he swayed on his feet. "I'm betting you let Horace have a taste," his sinister laugh sounded behind him as he made his exit.

Pearl let out an anguished gasp. Nervously she looked up at Louis. Louis flashed Pearl a cold stare.

She took a step back. A knot of apprehension seized her as tears filled her eyes. "Oh Louis, I can explain, everything that's been happening," she said nervously, not waiting for his response.

Her feelings were waging a war inside of her. She rubbed her brow. "I've been so stupid. Maybe I've experienced some sort of huge moral lapse. I don't know. But I've never cheated on you Louis, I swear," she said as her lips quivered. "All I know is that you are always so busy every year taking care of putting together the Grand Ball. You never have time for me. You never talked to me. Or…" Tears slowly rolled down her face. "Louis I'm so sorry, so sorry."

"Pearl," he breathed out in anguish. He shuddered at the thought of her ever leaving him. "You don't have to apologize. It is I who should apologize for neglecting you and always leaving you at home with children, waiting for me."

Louis pulled her close and brushed a kiss on her forehead. "God, I love you Pearl, more than you can ever know. There's so much I want to say to you. So much I want to do," he leaned his head and looked at her. "Like spending time making love to you," he said kissing her hard.

Abruptly he pulled apart. "I can't imagine my life without you. Promise me you'll never leave me," he hoarsely murmured.

His lips kissed hers again.

Pearl leaned into his kiss, content. Finally, Louis was saying things she wanted to hear. He loved her. "Of course, I'll never leave you, Louis," she murmured between kisses. "Why would you say something like that?"

Abruptly Louis ended the kiss and glanced back at her. "Because, right now I've got to get back to taking care of my duties for this ball," his eyes met hers. "Which means that I've got to abandon you again," he said in a soft tone.

Stunned by his truthfulness, Pearl's body gave a jolt. She stood there with her mouth open. All at once she threw back her head and laughed.

Louis watched her laugh. He was enthralled. It was good to see his Pearl laughing again. "What?" he asked bashfully amused. "You know I love only you Pearl. I promise I'll make it up to you, tonight after this blasted event is over with."

"You are one of a kind Louis. At least you told me, you loved me Louis. Promise me you won't change Louis," she hesitated. "Oh, and Louis, you will make this up to me tonight."

Immediately Louis reached out and grabbed her hand. "Come along wife. The Pageant's about to start, I'll walk you back. You can sit with Grand-mere Catherine and keep her company," he said.

Chapter 26

I've been looking for her...

Loud, boisterous clapping, and cheering erupted from the ballroom as Grand-mere Catherine and Pearl stood in the entrance of the massive framed doors. Spotlights directed the eyes to the performance on stage.

Pearl's eyes searched the stage looking for the two familiar faces. Finally, she saw them. The both stood poised and ready for the grand march.

She smiled and watched as her daughter Lacey nervously played with the ribbon on her dress. She gripped the basket of rose petals, ready to make her descent before the Junior Royal Court's final march down the center aisle.

Pearl shifted her glance and saw her son Nicholas standing proudly with his arm linked with Jade Mondragon. Standing behind Nicholas was his best friend Quinn Rolandis and Lucy Mondragon.

The Junior Royal marched off of the stage.

"Pearl and Grand-mere Catherine, I saved your seats," Mrs. Milady Egan said. "You've just made it in time to see the finale march of the Junior Royal Court."

"We saw the whole performance from the wings of the main door,"

Pearl assured her.

Grand-mere Catherine nodded. "Milady you look stunning."

Milady Egan was dressed elegantly. She wore a silk Hermes scarf tied fashionably around her head. It was pinned with a beautiful diamond and pearl cluster that gave it a crowning touch.

"Yes and your children too, if they need them," Milady nodded.

Pearl laughed softly. "Thanks, but I asked because, well, I think your son is headed this way," she said waiving her hand. "I wouldn't want that tall son of yours mad at me for taking his seat. The boy has to be six feet tall now. Why, I believe he will be taller than his father?"

"He is almost there now and he's only twelve and a half," Milady giggled softly.

At the mention of his name, twelve-year-old Kienan Egan headed toward them. His mesmerizing, piercing silver-gray eyes gleamed with youthful happiness.

"Hello everyone, I'm so excited about this night," his voice bubbled over and changed octaves several times.

Grand-mere Catherine looked up and tried not to laugh at the young boys changing voice. "Well…Well now look who's here."

"Grand-mere Catherine and Mother Pearl," Kienan greeted them cheerfully. "It's so good to see you both."

Grand-mere Catherine's hand rose tenderly and cupped his chin. "My goodness you're growing into a powerfully handsome young man Kienan. Give me a hug."

He did as he was told and put his arm around her.

"Hey Mrs. La Cour, don't forget my hug."

Pearl smiled. "You know Kienan; I think I love it best when you call me Mother Pearl."

Milady Egan beamed proudly at her son. He shared her slanted, hooded, almond-shaped, piercing, silver-gray eyes.

"Kienan is helping with the Jr Royal Court program. They asked him to be the announcer and introduce each entry," Milady proudly said.

A young man's changing voice sliced the air. "Kienan, dude did you save me a seat? Mr. Louis is about to crown the queen. I hope it's the girl with the big hooters."

Kienan frowned. "Hawke watch your language. There are ladies present. By the way, your voice, man, is changing again."

Hawke swallowed hard. "I'm sorry ladies," he said as he nervously turned and stared at the three pairs of eyes looking back at him. Shyly he ran his fingers through his curly brown hair.

Milady, Pearl and Grand-mere Catherine glanced between each other, as the young man took his seat. They all knew Hawke wasn't yet aware of how handsome he was. The boy had charisma. That star quality that Hollywood sought after. The kind that made you stand out and get noticed.

Hawke Deville flashed his most ravishing, charismatic, smile. "Hello Grand-mere Catherine, Mrs. Egan and Mrs. La Cour," he murmured in greeting them.

Pearl went to open her mouth in greeting. Instantly a young girl walked past giggling.

"Hi Hawke, you and Kienan were impressive on stage tonight," she giggled. "My friend Orchid said to tell you she has a crush on you," the girl said quickly before making a hasty exit.

Grand-mere Catherine nodded. "Hawke, you're growing into a handsome young man. I bet those green eyes of yours will break the hearts of many a young lady someday."

Hawke cocked his head to the side. "You think so?" He asked nudging Kienan and looking in the direction the girl went. "Kienan man, we should take advantage of intermission and make a run."

Kienan frowned and cleared his throat. "Alright, alright Ladies, we've got to make a quick run…Ah to the bathroom."

Hawke smiled a little and took the hint. "Yeah…Ah bathroom," he said hesitantly.

Kienan turned and winked at Grand-mere Catherine." We'll be right back Grand-mere Kat?"

Grand-mere Catherine chuckled and nodded. Her face broke into a genuine smile. "Well, Milady, maybe you and I should make a run for the lady's room, since it is intermission."

Milady nodded. "Yes, now is the time before the show starts," she said following after her.

At that moment from a short distance away, Pauline Baptiste waived her hand and slowly strode over. She glanced about nervously. "Pearl," she said urgently, as her eyes glanced at the empty seats in the row beside her.

Pearl vigorously eyed the empty seats at the end of the row. "I'm saving those seats for my family and Milady and her son Kienan and his friend," she blurted out. "They all just went to the bathroom," she said feeling the need to explain.

Pauline faintly smiled. "I'm not checking for seats Pearl. Have you seen Ming? I've been looking for her everywhere. I can't find her anywhere."

Pearl shook her head decisively. "No, I haven't seen her, and the Junior Court is already over. Maybe she's backstage seeing to her girls Lucy and Mimi," she suggested.

"No, I've checked," Pauline said waiving her hand helplessly.

Pearl looked back at Pauline strangely. "Is everything alright Pauline? You know I've had a bad feeling something might happen. I saw a bad moon rising."

Pauline arched a brow and snapped. "My goodness Pearl, you hang on to every old wives' tale of that Louisiana mumbo jumbo, don't you?"

"Excuse me Pauline," Pearl hissed. "I didn't mean to upset you with my old wives' tales," she said, staring intently at her. She could tell Pauline was upset about something. Still she wasn't going to be bullied by anyone.

A deep flustered expression crossed Pauline's brow. "I'm sorry for snapping at you like that Pearl. I hope I didn't offend you. I just have so much on my mind and I can't understand where Ming has disappeared to."

"It's okay Pauline, I'm fine," she said. She realized Pauline needed something to take her mind off of Ming.

The moments lingered between them.

After a long moment of silence Pearl felt the need to break the ice."Are you and Jean sitting together to watch Katrina compete in the Royal Queen's pageant?"

"Huh?" Pauline's thoughts were completely elsewhere as she glanced around the ballroom one more time. "At the moment, I'm more concerned about what happened to Ming. My daughter Katrina could care less about any advice I had to offer to her on winning the competition or losing it. As a matter of fact, she could care less if I was present," she said stiffly.

A shocked expression registered on Pearl's face.

Pauline breathed out a laugh. "Pearl, why do you look so surprised? I told you earlier I had daughter trouble."

There was a long silence between them.

"I won't keep you any longer Pearl. I must get going."

Pearl watched Pauline walk down the aisle toward the exit.

A short time later, Pauline looked around the lobby. For a moment she stood next to the empty bell hop desk. After a moment she strolled and made her way through to the main lobby door. It was dark outside, and it was late. But the fresh air felt good. She hoped it would help her clear her thoughts.

She walked down the sidewalk a few paces past the valet station. Cars were parked side by side under the huge grand portico. Gilded gold ornate columns gleamed under the overhead lighting. Mercedes Benzes, new Cadillac's, Jaguars and other expensive cars made the huge open space resemble a luxury car lot.

Out of the corner of her eyes she caught sight of two people talking behind the Valet Box. She had thought that the area was deserted. She stepped back behind one of the massive columns to get her bearing. She needed to be alone.

She looked around for a place to go. All at once she overheard the young men talking.

"That Katrina Baptiste is such a whore. I saw her going into that old fart Nate Trent's suite earlier today."

The other boy laughed.

She recognized the young man doing the talking. She'd seen him earlier that day. She peeked around the column. She watched as he pulled out a pack of cigarettes. He put one in his mouth and lit it.

He inhaled his cigarette and blew out smoke before he continued. "My oldest brother went to school with Jorge Manteau. Jorge told him Katrina was nothing but a whore."

The other boy just nodded and grinned wide. "Dude, I believe that. I like easy girls, but Katrina is too easy, so I hear."

"Yeah me too," the boy with the cigarette said while puffing away. "You know, I heard Jorge caught Katrina sleeping with her cousin Delilah Deauville."

"Oh really," the other boy said. "Now that's a bonafide whore. I heard Delilah used to be Conrad Mondragon's mistress. Did you know that?"

"What?" the boy with the cigarette grunted. "Dude I bet she still is. I saw her going up to the Mondragon suite earlier. Then his wife Ming went up."

All at once Pauline cleared her throat making her presence known. "What did you say?" Her voice sliced the air coldly as she startled the two young men.

"Pardon us Madam," the young man with the cigarette threw it down then crushed it under his foot. He adjusted his jacket and stood at attention. "My apologies Madam. We were just taking our break. We didn't know anyone was listening. We're just shooting off at the mouth. Please forgive us. Please don't report us Miss."

Pauline didn't know which issue to deal with first. She shook out her thoughts and realized her daughter Katrina's habits were greatly influenced by Delilah Deauville. And now they were just as notorious as she was. She shook her head. She had been aware of that fact for a very long time. She was starting to feel that Katrina needed to grow up and deal with the consequences of her actions. But Ming, sweet Ming didn't deserve to be mistreated. She had to find her.

Pauline looked hopeful as she stared back at the two young men and cleared her throat.

"I understand you don't want me to mention what you were talking about. Well, I'm willing to do that for you. If one of you can help me," her eyes darted nervously between them. "You see; I need to get into the Mondragon's suite."

One of the young men whistled loudly. "Lady, what you are asking could get us fired."

The moment was awkward. A strange silence hung in the air.

"Please, my friend could be hurt," she pleaded.

All at once the atmosphere changed abruptly. The smell of roses played on the air. Then a sound drifted by, like the rushing of the wind as it blew through reeds.

The woman seemed to have come out of thin air. "I can let you into the room. A red headed woman with large saucer-wide blue eyes stood there. She was dressed in the navy-blue blazer with the gold crest of the San Jose Hotel. There was strangeness about the young woman like she'd just stepped out of a dream.

Startled, Pauline jumped. She breathed out. "Oh, my goodness, I didn't see you walk up," she said in a shrill voice. She took a deep breath. "If you can help me, I would appreciate it. I'm just so worried," she said feeling an odd fluttering in her stomach.

The red headed woman had a dream like aura about her. But Pauline didn't care. If she could help her, all the better.

Minutes later Pauline got off of the elevator and the silent woman waved a key and opened the suite.

The suite was dark. Pauline immediately made her way to the bedroom.Instantly her hand made contact with the light switch and turned it on.

Ming lay naked, sprawled across the bed. "Ming…Ming…What have they done to you?" she cried roughly shaking her.

Pauline pressed her fingers into Ming's neck to feel for a pulse. She felt her heart beating.

"My God Ming, wake up!"

Slowly Ming opened her eyes. Abruptly she closed them.

"Ming look at me! Look at me!"

Pauline looked at her side. The silent woman was still standing there.

"Please help me. We need to get her into the shower."

They dragged Ming into the bathroom and put her in the shower. She ran the cold water on her.

Ming's shrill voice screamed.

Pauline laughed out. "That's right Ming scream for me baby. Welcome back to the land of the living."

Pauline turned to look back at the woman who had helped her carry Ming. The spot where the woman had stood was empty.

Chapter 27

And the winner is ...

Later that same night, the pageant finale' commenced. The small close-knit group watched as the reigning queen Sabrina St. Andre took her final march across the stage. She pivoted, spun around, and walked over and took her final seat on her thrown.

After a round of applause, Louis La Cour introduced the final three contestants. "Ladies and gentlemen, may I introduce to you the final three contestants for tonight's Grand Isles Christmas Ball.

Louis called their names. "Claire Marie Champagne, Katrina Baptiste and Prosperina Maeve Pascal," his voice announced boisterously.

The audience clapped thunderously as each name was called.

As each name was called, each one strutted confidently across the stage and took their place beside Louis.

An envelope was handed to Louis. His eyes gazed back at the audience.

Complete silence.

"And now folks, the moment we've all been wanting for," Louis struggled with the envelope. He opened it. "And the winner is…"

Louis' face didn't show emotion. "Prosperina Maeve Pascal!"

The audience went wild.

At that very moment, Katrina Baptiste scolded angrily watching former queen Sabrina relinquish her crown. She felt her stomach twist into knots as she looked on the new queen. Angry tears fell out of the corners of her eyes and streamed down her face. She kept her eyes on the crown.

Former queen Sabrina St. Andre closed the distance between her and Prosperina. She slowly took the crown off of her head and crowned Prosperina."

Prosperina Maeve Pascal's smile was wide as she took her walk as reigning queen. Her sleek long legs moved gracefully as she walked across the stage.She reached the end of the catwalk, pivoted and returned to centred stage.

Angry and defeated Katrina Baptiste didn't take her defeat lightly. She stepped in front of Prosperina. "This isn't fair!" her voice spits out with rage. "Bitch! That's my crown. I paid for that crown. It's mine," she yelled, pulling it off of her head.

"Girl fight!" Someone yelled from the audience.

Prosperina Maeve Pascal tilted back on her heels, her arms flapping. Instantly she grabbed Katrina's bodice of her dress. It ripped in their struggle.

"Look what you did you whore!" Katrina yelled.

Claire Marie Champagne pointed. "Damn, Katrina! What a liar you are. You're the whore. I heard you bragging you were going to sleep with one of the judges to ensure you won that crown. Well it looks like whoever it was you slept with played you for a fool!"

Chaos and laughter broke out in the audience.

"Bring the curtain down!" Louis yelled, taking control of the situation. "Ladies and gentlemen please return to the main ballroom. A Late-Night Buffet Dinner is now served."

"I want my mommy!" Katrina yelled, rushing off of the stage. She ran heading for the exit door and slammed it shut behind her.

"This entire night has been ruined," someone yelled.

An elderly lady with a purple hair rinse laughed out. "No, it wasn't!

This was the best drama spectacle I've ever seen!"

Chapter 28

When your lies catch up with you...

Pauline heard the door of the suite open and slam abruptly. Then she heard the loud sobs and knew.

"Mommy!"

She heard the tinge of sadness and regret laced in her daughter's voice. She knew without ever being told. Katrina's wild scheming and lies had caught up to her.

"Katrina baby I'm in the bedroom," she said warily, as she called out. She suppressed a sigh and braced herself for what she knew was coming. It was a mother's duty.

"Oh mom…Mom!" Katrina's face quivered and crumpled as she openly sobbed, rushing forward.

Pauline held out her arms as Katrina walked into their embrace and cried like a baby against her chest.

After a half-hour of tear wrenching soul searching that she finally realized had been totally self-inflicted, Katrina hiccupped and finally spoke. "Mom, I'm not angry with you. I'm angry at myself. I wanted to be the Royal Queen so bad that I was willing to do something stupid just to try and win."

Pauline listened to Katrina recant what had happened without comment. She nodded her head understandingly, as she reached and handed her a tissue.

Katrina stared blankly and thought. Everything was gone. All of her plans, she felt humiliated. "I guess if anything I should be glad you haven't passed judgment or told me you told me so," she quietly said and then blew her nose.

A serene expression clouded Pauline's eyes as she said. "At times we have all fallen from a high place we've put ourselves in of our own doing. But with strength we get back up again and move on."

"I know you're right."

Pauline's eyes locked with her daughter's, thoughtfully. She said a quick prayer. "It will be a great scandal when all of this reaches the news. I feel sorry for your father. He will feel the shame of it. He and his business," she muttered under her breath.

"Oh, what do you mean?"

She shrugged. "Oh, I can hide myself away at home, I don't work outside the house," Pauline said solemnly. "But your father has to take care of his business. Meet people, see his clients. He will bear a huge embarrassment in the community with his business," she sighed and continued.

It was a sad moment.

Katrina tilted her head and stared back in understanding.

Pauline nodded and continued. "Your father and I bare responsibility for having spoiled you without regarding the consequence," she said tenderly caressing her daughter's brow. She sighed heavily. "But your acknowledgment to me of your short comings and being adult enough to admit your guilt in this whole thing tells me we'd done a better job than we knew, raising you. I'm proud of you Katrina."

She hugged her.

Katrina listened to her mother attentively. Slowly she came to the realization of what her deeds had subjected her family to. Abruptly, she pulled out of her mother's embrace.

"Do you really think the news people will care about what happened at this event?" she frowned. "And what do you mean this will be a scandal for father's business?"

"Oh yes. News is news, they will care. The more tantalizing and smuttier it is, the better," she paused. "Yes Katrina, you will probably make the front page of the Valley News. And yes it could affect you father's business. You can never know how some people will take the news."

A horrible thought entered Katrina's mind as she thought about the huge mistake she had made. She blinked rapidly trying to think of what to do to make things right. "I need to go to the bathroom," she said trying to get a hold of her thoughts.

At the bathroom door she stopped abruptly and stared. Ming Mondragon sat at the vanity in a dreamlike state. She jerked her head around and glanced back at her mother. That was the moment she noticed her mother's suitcases packed.

"Mom," she frowned. "Why is Ming sitting at the Vanity mirror staring into space and why are your bags packed?"

Pauline rose off of the bed and closed the distance between them. "I forgot I left Ming sitting there while I packed."

She delicately took Ming's hand. "Ming darling, please come sit on the bed and wait for me," Pauline said in a soft voice.

Katrina stared mouth wide as Ming walked from the bathroom as if held in a fog.

"Mom, what happened to Ming?"

Pauline's facial expression grew tense. "I'm not prepared to say, as I don't know the full truth yet," she said in a voice that seemed far away. "Don't worry about Ming. I'm going to take her home with me. I'll take care of her and I'll ask Mother Kahina Laveau to let Lucy and Mimi stay at her home a few days.

Katrina studied Ming. "But I bet you have your suspicions," she muttered under her breath. She thought about her cousin. Delilah Deauville, she could see her hand in this.

"Mom, you take care of Ming. Don't worry about me. Take Ming home and do whatever you need to take care of her. I'll take care of things here for you," she said assuredly. "Don't worry about your luggage. I'll make sure the bellboy comes and gets it. I'll make sure everything gets taken care of."

Pauline's eyes lit up. "Oh, would you? Then I'll take Ming to the car now."

A few minutes later, Katrina stood under the grand portico and closed the car door soundly.

She watched as her mother started the car and pulled away.

All at once the wind howled and blew a chill.

Out of the corner of her eye Katrina thought she saw something. She jerked her head around and looked back through the front door of the hotel and shivered.

Chapter 29

❧

**A diabolical mastermind or a monster-
hell-bent on destroying the lives of everyone...**

Louis couldn't remember the last time he'd encountered such an embarrassing situation. It was time he tried to get all the sordid details of this disaster cleared up, he thought.

"Hey Louis, that was some show," a little old man exclaimed. He was wearing white spats over his shoes. They made him look old-fashioned. He patted Louis on the back. "I wouldn't have seen that much action if I had stayed at home and watched boxing on TV."

Louis focused ahead and kept walking. He was determined to reach the judges box before anyone had time to leave.

The crush of the crowd seemed overwhelming as Louis pushed his way through.

"Louis, we've got a big problem, a big problem!" Clare Palling said, rushing to catch up with him.

"Yeah, I already know," Louis grunted.

"We've got to find out who the man was that Katrina slept with. He compromised his position. Not to mention the integrity of what this event stands for."

At that moment a stout man in a military jacket intercepted them. He heralded his voice like a hand grenade. "Louis, I'm Colonel Beauvoir," he drenched out through an alcoholic breathy mist, as his body swayed showing he had too much to drink. "And what are you going to do about this embarrassing situation?'

Louis tilted his head and took a step back. The man's breath was powerful. "Rest assured I'm working on it."

Louis quickly put some distance between him and the man.

Clare Palling caught up with him and grabbed his arm. "Louis stop. We need to talk. What are you going to do about this situation?"

Abruptly Louis stopped walking turned and gave her his attention. "I'm on my way to confront Nate Trent right now and make him come to an emergency meeting, immediately."

"It has to be a closed session," she suggested. "We'd hate for anyone to discover that we let a diabolical mastermind run amok though our Grand Gala Ball!"

"I was thinking we were just dealing with a monster hell bent on destroying the lives of everyone connected to the Gala," Louis condescendingly stated.

"Now, Louis, let's not squabble over what name we call this spineless feign, the question is how are you going to handle him!" Eagerly Clare looked around. "We don't want to draw any more attention to this situation."

"I know," Louis nodded. "It will be a discreet closed session," he nodded. "This is an embarrassing situation for everyone. The closed session will at least allow us to determine what public statement we will make, once we assess the damage," he stopped abruptly. "And we can decide immediately if we will end the Royal Queen Pageant tonight and forever. We've got to do this so that this doesn't tarnish the foundations reputation in the community."

"You'll do no such thing," a man's voice barrelled out.

"Ulysses," Louis said drily. "Didn't you just witness what happened? One of our pageant contestants and one of our judging panel may have slept together."

Ulysses' jowls quivered. "Yes…Yes… I heard. But Louis don't be foolish," he paused. "The attorney in me won't have you running off and causing us any unnecessary lawsuits."

Louis and Clare slowly looked between each other.

Clare breathed out slowly. "He's right Louis. I wasn't thinking about lawsuits. What do you propose that we should do Ulysses?"

Ulysses rubbed his hands together. "Since this is an embarrassing situation, I think we should call a private closed session emergency meeting as soon as possible with the girl and her parents and see what they want done," he said. "I just thank God the girl was eighteen."

"That's not what you should be afraid of," a man's voice replied.

The small party turned and stared as David Creek walked into the circle.

He came and stood in front of them. "You three have been so worried about keeping this embarrassing situation hushed up that you forgot about our little Miss Victim Katrina."

"Okay, what do you mean," Louis said.

"I mean our little victim went straight to that TV news crew."

The moment was tense.

"Really?" Louis piped in. "How do you know?"

Clare whistled through her teeth. "Well hot damn, the drama fest will really begin now."

David shrugged. "I know, because I saw her in the lobby with him just minutes ago."

Ulysses threw his head back and laughed.

It was an awkward moment.

"Ulysses, what's so funny?" David asked.

He shrugged confidently. "I didn't think the girl had the gumption. She's a lot more intelligent than I thought. Or not."

Louis shot him a puzzled look. "Ulysses, you're not worried?"

"No," Ulysses shook his head and his jowls moved.

Clare nudged Louis. The two of them stared between each other. She leaned over and whispered. "Well, at least the girl can't say the guy took her virtue. I've heard that Katrina has been a busy little girl when it comes to knowing about the birds and the bees."

Silently, the small party stared among themselves.

<h1 style="text-align:center">Chapter 30</h1>

Calm in the throngs of chaos…

Pearl found a quiet corner off in the romantic garden off of the ballroom.

The twinkling blinking lights and the romantic ambiance made the room a safe haven. She found a spot and sat and exhaled slowly.

All of the couples had deserted the area. No doubt because of the late-night Buffet Dinner.

A short distance away, Celica Baptiste watched Pearl sitting alone. She closed the distance between them.

"Pearl, how can you sit so calmly through the throngs of that chaos taking place inside?" she boldly asked but didn't wait for a response. "Do you mind if I sit down for a second?"

"No, not at all," Pearl shrugged. She quickly glanced up at her. She noted the drink in her hand. In fact, Celica looked like she had been drinking for a long time. The bottle she carried in her other hand was the tip-off. She also noticed she no longer wore the loud hot pink dress she had on earlier.

Celica's hair had been neatly brushed back into a tight bun at the top of her head. She wore a black satin pants outfit with a Kimono styled duster.She looked elegant with a fatally cold sophisticated aura about her.

"Excuse me for a moment," Celica said as she downed her drink in one gulp.

Pearl nodded and watched her pour another one. She tried to read the label on the bottle. Celica's hand was covering it. "What's that you're drinking Celica, if you don't mind my asking?"

Celica grinned. "I call it a white-hot mess. Want to know how I made it?" she asked but didn't wait for a reply. "I filled up a rum bottle with three different kinds of liquor all by myself," her voice was slurred. "First I had to sort of empty the bottle. So, I drank half the white rum. I drank it all by myself," she repeated through giggles. "Then I added some white gin, white tequila, and white vodka," she giggled again. "It tastes delicious, I think."

A saucy laugh escaped her mouth.

Pearl could tell that she had a few too many.

In one breath Celica said. "Pearl, there's so much I want to say to you. I respect and like you as a friend," she slurred out.

Pearl gazed back at her with wide eyes. The moment was awkward.

Celica blinked back tears. "There is so much I need to explain..." she shook her head as if trying to clear her thoughts. "Oh God Pearl I know a secret," she said gloomily. "Monty Wildfire is in love with you. He told me so himself. But that's not the worst of it."

"Oh," Pearl declared.

Silence fell. The air was chilled.

Pearl was afraid to ask any questions. She stared back at Celica, puzzled.

"Monty's nothing but a lying, manipulative, vindictive bastard. He's determined to break up your marriage Pearl. He all but told me so. He thinks Louis isn't good enough for you and that he is," her words tumbled out. "Pearl you've got to do something to protect yourself or God knows what he'll do. You've got to tell Louis!"

Pearl smiled softly and reached over and touched Celica's hand. "Thank you for being my friend Celica and for telling me about Monty.

But I already found that out," she nodded. "Oh, and Louis has dealt with the situation," she added.

"Really?"

Pearl looked back at Celica. She looked like a child that needed reassuring. "Yes, he has. And I'm sure Monty took Louis very seriously."

Slowly a satisfied expression crossed Celica's face. "Good...Good...," her voice was low. "I'm so glad to hear that."

Pearl gave Celica a long considering look. "Celica, do you ever think of finding another job?" she asked. "I mean stop working for Monty."

"No!" she exclaimed. "No, there is no reason to," she said, with a completely calm face.

The moment was awkward.

Celica's eyes glazed over as she stared off into the distance. "I'm sure Monty underestimated Louis' love for you. And I'm sure Louis taught Monty a valuable lesson," she said starting to leave. "Everything has been taken care of, that's good... Nope, I don't need to look for a new job."

Pearl looked anxiously back at her, trying to get a clue as to what she was thinking. "Celica are you alright?" she asked with deep concern.

Celica stood. "I'm fine...I'm fine," she laughed out strangely. "I'll leave you now. You and Louis should be happy now," she said, as she slowly walked away.

Chapter 31

✧❦✧

The Truth & the Whole Truth... I swear...

Clare Palling folded her arms. "I always said this should be a Debutante ball," she remarked with a stern expression. "That way we'd have less chance of a scandal as it would eliminate the need for judges' altogether. And the girls would only be allowed to wear a long formal ball gown all evening. For sure we would preserve the fairy-tale myth."

Louis was exasperated. "Well, right now we don't have a stupid fairy tale. We've got real life happening all around us. We need to get Katrina and get her out of here fast!"

Ulysses stared across the room and then murmured low under his breath. His eyes darted quickly between his two friends. "That is a great suggestion. However, due to the urgency, I think we'd better come up with a bold face lie right about now to cover ourselves and this organization."

"What? We can't do a cover-up," Louis said. Then he took the hint and followed his gaze. "Damn," he muttered under his breath.

A few steps in front of them Katrina Baptiste was racing toward them.

Following close behind her was Horace Garrison wearing a solemn expression.And taking up the rear was Claire Marie Champagne.

Both Katrina and Claire Marie were dressed professionally in black business attire.

"Horace," Louis called. "What are you doing here?"

"I'm here as a friend and a reporter," Horace said nodding. "As a matter of fact, Katrina and Claire Marie gave me an interesting story that I've already sent into the station."

"What?" Louis blurted.

Katrina prayed for strength as she rushed forward. She wore a skirt suit with black patent three-inch pumps that made her look taller than her five-ten height. She radiated a professional, confident image.

"Yes…Yes, I did," she breathed out slowly. "I'm glad I caught everyone, so I won't have to say this but once," she paused. "Just so you know, I've made a statement to the press, regarding the so-called rumor that I slept with one of the judges," she said rolling her eyes in the direction of Claire Marie Champagne. "I have made it clear that it was a bold-faced lie brought on by circumstances out of my control." She hesitated to let her words sink in. "I apologize for the embarrassment this caused the Grand Isle Ball and my witness collaborates my story. You can ask Horace."

Horace cleared his throat and nodded his head affirmably. "Yes, it seems Claire Marie has recanted her earlier statement," he said.

"Well! Tell them Claire Marie!" Katrina demanded impatiently.

Claire Marie stood solemnly a foot behind Katrina. She looked drab in her pantsuit. Her hair was pulled tight into the nape of her neck. It made her ears stick-out profoundly. Her eyes were red, as if she'd been crying. She knew she was being manipulated. But she'd taken a risk, gambled on a man's love and lost badly.

The moment was awkward as she stared back at all of the stern serious faces looking at her. She felt confused and unsure of herself for a brief moment and then her expression changed as she remembered. She had been bought off with a price and an expectation. Taking the money meant she had to say it. She held her head high and said. "Yes, Katrina is right. I recanted my story," she said firmly as she looked up at Katrina with a strange expression. They knew they shared a secret.

The moment was awkward.

Claire Marie kept her gaze focused in the distance as she spoke. "I came here with Katrina to make a statement for the press because…Because it is the right thing to do," Claire Marie's voice trailed off. Her thoughts raced as she stared between the faces standing in front of her. She knew why she'd come. Katrina was a little blackmailer who had pictures of her sleeping with Jorge Manteau. She didn't know which was worse, calling someone a whore or finding out the boy that you thought you'd been seeing had been playing you for one. As far as she was concerned Jorge Manteau and Katrina Baptiste deserved each other. They were two of a kind. But that wasn't what she'd come there to share.

Claire Marie cleared her throat. "In a fit of jealousy and anger I may have said something that wasn't true. When I said Katrina was sleeping with one of the pageant judges. I lied, because I was angry and upset that I didn't win the pageant," her words rushed out as she confessed. It felt good to say it even though the shocked faces staring back at her made her feel like a prisoner on trial.

She swallowed hard and continued. "Anyway, this was all just a big misunderstanding. And I apologize for what I said and for any embarrassment I've brought onto this wonderful worthy event and the pageant. I am truly sorry," she added dryly.

Ulysses' face was set in a terrifying mask as his jowls shook. "It was malicious and ill thought out," he blurted out. "This may have done irrevocable harm to Grand Isle Ball, not to mention the illustrious organization it stands for."

Claire Marie's eyes glazed over with an expression of sadness. Her chest was so tight that she could hardly breathe as she asked. "Ulysses, have you ever been in love?" she choked out as her eyes glistened with tears.

Louis cleared his throat as he leaned in close and looked Ulysses in the eye. "That was just a little harsh," he said tersely.

Clare Palling took a step forward and took over the situation. "Thank you for telling us your statements Claire Marie and Katrina. I know it took courage for both of you to come forth and do the right thing after that ignominious catastrophe earlier," she said with a nod of her head.

She turned her attention. "And Katrina, thank you for discovering the truth. I'm sure your statement to the press will do a world of justice for this organization," she said assuring them. "If you and Claire Marie are finished you may go."

Claire Marie pivoted and walked away quickly. It was obvious she didn't want to leave with Katrina.

The small group watched as Katrina walked away in the opposite direction.

Clare Palling broke the ice. "So, Horace, what did you say in your story? How did you use the girl's statements? Did you defuse it?"

"No, I didn't have to defuse it. Nor did I have to write the story. The girls wrote their own story and it was brilliant and worth publishing. It was apologetic, sincere and thought provoking. It told the tale of two girls in love with the same man, and how the guy betrayed both of them by using them both for his perverse desire to have two beautiful women in love with him at the same time; without either one knowing about the other"

Clare laughed. "Sounds like a soap opera to me."

"I don't care what it sounds, like just so long as it exonerates the foundation," Louis blurted.

"Are you sure their story held the foundation blameless?" Ulysses asked.

Horace shrugged. "I'm sure it did. Like I said, those two girls know how to write a story and the public will eat it up and love it. And I don't feel there will be any repercussions from it for the event or the organization."

"Well, thank God for that," Louis said running his fingers through his hair in relief. He sighed out heavily. "I'm going to go to my suite and be with my wife. I don't want this to sound rude but I don't want anyone calling me for anything," he said turning and walking away.

Horace cleared his throat. "I'll be leaving too," he said with a nod.

Clare and Ulysses watched him go.

She linked her arm with his. "Well, Ulysses, as I recall, last year the two of us were left alone at the end of the ball and you agreed to be my drinking buddy."

He chuckled. "And as I recall, you enjoyed our doing so. However, Ms. Claire Palling, this year I'm afraid I have to add some ground rules."

"What? Ground rules for drinking? You're not serious?" she asked.

"Yes I am. Every year at the end of this event you need a drinking partner; but throughout the year I need a companion. So, I feel, if I'm good enough to drink with once a year, I'm good enough to drink with all year long. So, what do you say?"

"Ulysses you're asking me to go steady with you, how sweet."

"Go steady! Woman if we can get along a whole year, we're getting married. Hell, we should get married at the Grand Isle Ball next year because I know we're going to make it."

Clare snuggled in close. "So where are we drinking tonight? Your room or mine?"

"I've got Bourbon for me and martini mixers for you, up in my room?"

Clare smiled wide. "Then your room it is."

Chapter 32

There are those who meddle...

A few minutes later, Catherine Marie Rousseau-Andries La-Cour walked away from the reception desk and took the elevator and made her way to the fifteenth floor.

Her footsteps were hushed as she walked on the luxurious carpet. Her face flushed as she neared the suite Remington Breaux was staying in.

Nervously she reached inside of her purse for the key. She fumbled furiously, trying to locate the key.

Behind her she heard a man's laughter. Recognition hit her and abruptly she dropped her purse.

Within seconds the man rounded the corner. He wasn't alone.

"Ah! Catherine," the man breathed out as shock registered.

"Catherine what are you doing there on the floor?"

The moment was awkward as she looked back at her sister.

Just then the door to the suite opened. "I thought I heard something. Catherine what are you doing on the floor?" he asked helping her up.

Delta's shrill voice laughed out. "Oh my God, Remington Breaux! You and my sister Saint Catherine, you two weren't about to sleep together?"

Embarrassed, Catherine clicked her tongue disapprovingly. "Shut your mouth Delta Dawn Allemande," Catherine said retrieving her items and closing her purse. "My personal business does not concern you!" she shot her sister a warning glance.

Delta giggled under her breath.

"Catherine, just ignore them and come into the room. They look like they were up to having their own sex machine party," Remington said.

Catherine studied the man her sister was hugged up next to. "Remington, you are certainly right," she softly smiled.

Catherine glanced around. Introductions were in order in keeping with the situation.

"By the way Remington you remember my sister Delta Dawn and this upstanding citizen she is hugged so close with is Professor Percy Newhouse."

Remington cleared his throat and nodded.

Professor Newhouse's smug smile greeted them. "Pleased to meet everyone."

Catherine saw her chance to get her sister back for embarrassing her. "Yes professor, it's good to meet you too. Do tell me, do you like to be called professor? Or would you like to be referred to by one of my sister Delta's pet names for you."

Flustered Delta shook her head and knew she had that one coming. "Oh no, I'll save those little tasty morsels for when we are alone." She leaned over close to her sister and whispered in her ear. "I think I should let you get to it old girl. It's been so long since you had sex you may need to warm up the internal fires awhile first," she joked. "Oh, and sister, if you have any questions about what to do with Remington just come next door. We're in the suite next to you."

"How wonderful," Catherine said sarcastically taking Remington's arm and leaving them standing there.

Chapter 33

Never drink with your worst enemy…

On the way back to her suite Celica's brain clicked in motion. The idea had been coming to her. It was clear now.

She entered her suite and walked straight to the desk that held the telephone.

Her hand trembled as she picked up the receiver and dialed the number.

"Delilah? It's me Celica.

"Celica, oh yeah, where's Monty?"

Celica's stomach flip-flopped at the sound of her hoarse nasal voice. "I don't know."

"What do you mean you don't know? You're Monty's assistant, aren't you?" Delilah commanded not waiting for an answer. "You're supposed to know where he is at all times," she ordered.

"Yes, you're right," she said feeling her chin tremble. "Look, I'm sorry. But Monty left strict instructions for me to call him if I heard back from you…"

Delilah's voice softened. "Oh, never mind. Celica did you, setup that appointment I wanted with Monty?"

"Yes, but Monty was hoping you'd have time right now. Since that crazy incident with the pageant, he figured you were still up and maybe he could meet and talk with you tonight?"

"Sure, I'm up. Call and tell Monty to drop by," she demanded into the phone," she hesitated. "Oh, and Celica, you come with Monty. We may need you to take some notes."

"What was that?" Celica asked.

"Yeah I said take some notes," Delilah snorted out the words with a sinister chuckle.

"Okay," Celica replied. She shivered at the sound of her voice. It made her sick in the stomach.

"That cat fight tonight was great wasn't it?" Delilah said with apparent interest. "Celica, get Monty over here as soon as possible. You hear me!" She demanded and laughed out again.

Just as quickly as Delilah's laughter started it abruptly ended, as she rudely slammed down the telephone in Celica's ear, ending the call.

"You devil bitch," Celica hissed into the dead telephone. "You are truly one damaged human being," she said, picturing Delilah licking her claws, sharpening them and readying them for her next prey.

Celica hung up the phone and stared at it. Convincing Monty Delilah wanted to meet with him wasn't going to be hard. She knew Monty thought Delilah was sexy and good looking. She'd seen him lick his lips, greedily eyeing her on many occasions.

He wouldn't pass up a chance to lick Delilah's milk bowl clean if she wanted him to.

She quickly dialed Monty's number.

Delilah Deauville private suite on the top floor of the San Jose hotel resembles an ancient Roman house, complete with a center huge skylight that opens to the sky.

Celica watched as Delilah swam in a miniature kidney shaped pool. Miniature wasn't the correct word for the pool's description, Celica thought. A few people could swim easily in it.

Delilah loved to live rich. The furniture layout of the room showed her desire for the extravagant. With its stunning gold ornate leaf design, magnificent Roman seating area complete with scatter cushions and a canopy secluded area known as a "lover's playpen" that was covered in flowing loose silk drapes. It was a lush paradise oasis for lovers.

Delilah studied Celica as she took it all in.

Celica spotted a cream colored, gorgeous, roman style lounge chaise complete with a carved marble base. The chair reminded her of a chair from her childhood. There had been one similar to it in Delilah's room when she was a girl. It was so similar she felt the need to sit in it.

From her seat Celica watched as Delilah enjoyed herself swimming about. She swam to the end of the pool and then stepped out, unashamed of her nakedness. She stepped over into the hot tub that lay at the end of the pool.

"What are you looking at?" Delilah asked then followed her gaze. "Oh, I see; you've remembered that chair. Or the one I had like it in my room."

Delilah had been born with the good looks in the family. The Hollywood glamorous kind that men fought over in the movies. She leaned against the side of the hot tub with her perfectly shaped full breasts exposed above the water.

Celica sat in silence and watched her as her thoughts preyed upon her. Her mind wondered back to a time long ago.

Celica thought she looked like the perfect statue of *Venus de Milo* with her perfect good looks outside and her cold as stone inside.

The two were more than ten years apart.

Delilah stole another glance at Celica. Her heart softened with the thought of her memories. She remembered when Celica had been born. She knew Celica was wondering where she fit in. Why the two of them had no resemblance. "Celica, when you look like that it makes me regret not trying to be close to you. Not trying to be a big sister."

"I never asked you to be my big sister."

Delilah felt the need to talk. It was rare that the mood hit her as she said. "Haven't you ever wondered why I don't resemble you?"

"Sometimes?"

Talking to Celica was like talking to a brick wall, Delilah thought. "You were always a quiet strange child Celica," she leaned back and studied her. "I used to think you had some kind of problem with memory issues or some kind of suppression syndrome," Delilah softly said. "Sometimes, I couldn't believe how calm you remained. Especially after that first time you caught that sick twisted father of yours in bed having sex with me. You were four years old and you ran out of the room and told your mommy. She whacked you on the bottom and told you to stay out of my room when your father was having a discussion with me. A discussion," she laughed out. "That's what she used to call his sexual romps with me."

Enraged, Celica turned and stared at her. "He was your father...I mean your step-father. Mother told me so when I asked her as I got older."

Anger flashed in Delilah's eyes. "He wasn't my father and he wasn't my stepfather," she said, her voice laced with anger. "And you still don't get the major problem here. Your mother didn't stop him from coming to my room."

"Mother said you two had a lot to discuss. That was why father always went to your room. She said he was laying the groundwork telling you about all the property you would be inheriting. That was why you were left all that money and property when he died."

"Oh really. That controlling strict bitch of a mother had an answer for that too. What a liar she was."

"Our mother was a self-sacrificing woman."

"She was a lying bitch of a hypocrite and she wasn't our mother. She was your mother," Delilah hissed. "I told you many times before not to believe a word she said," she looked at her strangely.

The two of them exchanged glances.

Delilah stared at her a moment longer and realized the only way she could wake Celica up from her fog was to tell her the truth.

Up until that moment, Delilah had kept it all hidden. The way she had felt frightened, helpless, demoralized and scared. Not when she first learned that her own drug addicted mother had sold her into slavery with the promise of a better life. But when she'd learned the hard way that she had been brought into that beautiful home to take care of the needs of the man she was to call her father after he'd crawled into her bed one night. Soon after, she was told firsthand by the woman she called mother, Pandora Deauville. That it was what was expected of her.

Delilah remembered sitting on the brand-new pink and white four poster canopied bed when Pandora opened her bedroom door and entered. She promised her anything she wanted if she would be good to him for her. She hated the woman they called mother.

She laughed out remembering. "Celica you're afraid to learn the truth."

"What the hell are you talking about?"

"Don't you know your mother knew he was sleeping with me?"

The shock of it made Celica's mouth drop open. She stared back into Delilah's eyes. She knew it was true. Flash backs of memories pressed upon her mind. She remembered what her mother had said just before she died. Tell Delilah I'm sorry for what I let her father and me do to her. Ask her to please forgive me....

Delilah realized Celica was thinking over everything she had said.She could tell she knew she was telling the truth.

Everything was still and quiet.

A short time later, Delilah's voice broke the ice as if nothing had happened. "When is Monty coming?" she asked.

At that precise moment there was a knock on the door.

"That must be him. I'll get it," Celica said, leisurely shaking her head and waking up out of her thoughts. She walked briskly toward the door.

Her thoughts raced. It would give her a chance to make sure her plan was in order. She picked up one of the bottles of champagne she had brought with her and grabbed three glasses before opening the door.

Monty was surprised to see her. "Hello Celica. I see you got the champagne ready.

Celica looked at his face. She quickly made sure Monty wouldn't have a chance to tell her she was dismissed. She let her voice fill the air. "Delilah, Monty is here."

Delilah giggled loudly. "Hi Monty, she yelled. "Come on back."

Celica motioned her hand for Monty to follow her. "Delilah is in the hot tub now. She's waiting for you. And she's naked," she hoarsely said.

The expression on Monty's face was one of wide happy glee as he ignored Celica and headed further into the suite.

She quickly followed behind him. She walked over and sat down the glasses, opened the bottle and poured their drinks.

When Delilah saw Monty, the first thing she did was stand up in the hot tub. She knew she looked good. Her body was firm and toned in all the right places men loved. Her body was made for giving men pleasure. "Monty you're here," she said motioning him to come closer.

Monty stood in front of her and loosened his shirt collar. He was thoroughly enjoying the view of the naked woman standing in front of him.

"Celica bring over those drinks," Delilah called trustingly.

Realization dawned on Monty as he stared back at Celica's backside, as she poured their drinks.

"Celica, you can leave after you bring us our drinks," he said.

"No. I want her to stay," Delilah said abruptly.

Celica did as she was told and handed them their drinks.

Startled by Delilah's directness Monty downed his drink. It went down smooth. The drink gave him courage. "Do you mind if I ask you why you want Celica to stay," he asked not taking his eyes off Delilah.

Immediately Delilah laughed and downed her drink. "Don't you know that Celica Baptiste and I are half-sisters?"

"What?" Monty looked puzzled between them.

"Not only that, we are sibling cousins," Delilah said as her eyes flickered with amusement.

Embarrassed, Celica lowered her head.

"Didn't Celica tell you that I'm her big sister? My father was the older of two brothers. Our mother, Pandora Baptiste, was married to my father for fifteen years until he died. When he died, he left me most of his money," she paused for effect. "Except a small part that he gave to my uncle, his younger brother. Pandora had secrets and she loved money. Of course, our mother married the younger brother, why not she was sleeping with him while she was married to his older brother. Celica is his child. Therefore, she is both my sister and my cousin."

The moment was silent.

Now that the truth was out, Celica kept quiet, with her head down.

"Come Celica, pour us another drink," Delilah commanded. It was obvious she was used to giving Celica orders.

Monty gulped down his drink and held out his glass.

Celica studied them as she poured both another drink. She watched attentively as the both wasted no time finishing their third drink.

"How do you feel Monty?" Celica asked but didn't wait for him to answer. "I mean aren't you feeling hot. Wouldn't you like to take off your clothes?"

"Yes…I believe I would."

Celica let her fingers do the work as she quickly helped him out of his clothes.

Monty leaned his head back looking up at the sky. "Ahhhh that feels better. I feel like I'm one with the world."

He stared back at Delilah. They were now both naked. As naked as the day they were born.

Delilah threw back her drink. "Well…Well, Monty, I had heard you were well formed. And it looks like they didn't lie."

"Celica, pour me another drink. I feel greedy," Delilah purred.

Celica noted it was Delilah's fourth drink. She was starting to lose count.

Then Delilah slowly she licked her lips and let her eyes trail down Monty's body. She checked out the hard erection between his legs. Her eyes looked up at him.

"Damn you swell up quickly Monty. I like that," Delilah giggled, closing the distance between them she kissed him hard and let her hands cup his member.

Celica turned to leave.

"Where are you going?" Delilah commanded. "Come and join us. And give me that bottle of champagne. I want to pour it on Monty and lick it off."

Celica looked between the two of them. Their inhibitions were dissolving. Their eyes held a cloudy faraway look. She smiled softly knowing her plan was working well.

She took her time closing the distance between them.

Slowly she handed the bottle of champagne to Delilah.

Delilah knelt down in front of Monty and poured. "I'm going to lick you Monty with my tongue."

The two went at it like rabbits as she watched them.

Celica smiled softly. Everything was finally good in her world. It was going as she planned. Soon she could leave them and neither one would notice her going.

Just at that moment a strange cloudiness passed over the skylight.

Startled Celica jerked, feeling a cold tickling sensation against her arm.

She looked up at Delilah and Monty. They were still going at it hard. They didn't even notice her.

Out of the corner of her eye Celica thought she saw a light flash. She had the weirdest feeling.

Speechless, she paused and sniffed the air. She thought she smelled roses and something else. It was a pleasurable scent. Like something from her childhood. It was something nurturing and reassuring. And then a strange, radiant and luminous, golden light appeared and so did a woman with flaming red hair.

"Celica," the red headed woman seemed to call her name but didn't speak the words.

Startled, she took a step back. She had never really believed in the supernatural stuff she saw in movies. "Who are you?" she whispered.

The woman looked past her.

Celica followed her gaze. She was staring at Monty and Delilah. Delilah was straddling Monty making love.

"You haven't thought this through," the woman said. "You must drink some of the champagne too."

"What?"

"You forget someone knows you had access to Monty's personal stash of champagne. If you don't drink some and get sick too, then someone may believe you drugged them."

Celica thought hard. When Monty saw her at the door, he hadn't even noticed the bottle of champagne with his signature label on it. It came from his personal stash.

Now she realized the flaw in her plan.

The woman seemed to float over and take hold of one of the unopened bottles of champagne.

Celica was amazed at how quickly she opened the bottle of champagne and poured.

The woman handed her the glass. "This way, in the morning, when the three of you are discovered by the maid, the manager of the hotel will call an ambulance to rush the three people to the hospital."

"You're right," Celica nodded with a wide-eyed stare. Her thoughts raced. Then Monty would be discovered as the person who gave us the Rohypnol. She hadn't thought of that.

She smiled with her thoughts and sipped slowly. She only had to take in a very insignificant amount of it just to make sure everything pointed to Monty.

She was sure Delilah would remember she told her the champagne was a gift from Monty.

She watched them and slowly sipped. She felt relaxed.

Chapter 34

Your worst enemy...

Conrad Mondragon thought he had slept like a baby.

Suddenly hands were shaking his shoulders.

"Conrad…Conrad. Wake up," a woman's voice called.

He pushed back against the pillow and slowly opened his eyes.

Duchess Lanchow was shaking him. She brushed her glossy black hair. "Madame Lemieux will return soon. You need to leave."

Conrad was exhausted and satisfied. Excellent sex always made him feel on top of the world. "Tell her I'll pay her extra just to sleep a little longer. Come back to bed with me Duchess. What do you say?"

"No Mr. Mondragon I want you to leave now."

He yawned. "No..," he protested sleepily.

Conrad never saw the fear that etched its way slowly across Duchess Lanchow's face. Her eyes abruptly gazed at the door.

A loud thunderous boom roared as the door was kicked open.

Conrad's eyes shot open.

Duchess immediately ran out of the door.

"You, dumb bastard! Get your horny ass out of that bed! It's me. Your worst enemy, you remember, you're fucking brother-in-law," his voice said tersely.

"Leroy!"

Leroy Maddox Jefferson was Ming's older brother.

A passionate anger rose across Leroy's face as he closed the distance between them and threw off the sheets. Immediately his hand jerked out and made contact with Conrad's head.

Conrad could feel the intense pain of having been hit by Leroy. Leroy Maddox Jefferson had been a tough street wise kid from the time he could pour milk on his cereal.

"Damn!" Conrad said feeling the pain of his punch as he crawled out of bed.

He sat on the floor and nursed his face.

Leroy Maddox Jefferson was slant eyed square-jawed, handsome, muscle bound, and tall. He stayed close to his Oakland roots. As a young kid he taught a neighbour gangster how to make money on the stock market. The gangster did. He made millions and he rewarded the young genius by sending him to UC Berkley. Leroy held a degree in finance from UC Berkley. He was an educated stock market guru and a bonafide hoodlum thug.

"Leroy, I forgot you were a man of few words. What are you doing here?" Conrad asked rubbing his jaw as he rose.

Leroy laughed out maliciously. "I missed seeing my brother-in-law. Can't you see I came here to show you some love?"

Conrad got the feeling Leroy was lying but didn't want to press the issue.

Leroy smiled and Conrad tried to crack a smile back at him. His face hurt.

Finally, Leroy spoke. "Do you have anything you want to tell me Conrad?"

Conrad shrugged following his gaze looking around the room. "Oh this?" he asked but didn't' wait for a response. "This isn't what you think it is," he paused. "Okay, maybe it is what you think.But what if I told you Ming knows I'm here and she doesn't have a problem with my getting a little on the side."

Leroy glared at him. "Get dressed brother-in-law we need to take a ride."

Fifteen minutes later, they made their way through the lobby of the hotel. Outside, the sky was dark. It had to be after four o'clock in the morning.

The limousine driver stood by the car door and opened it.

Conrad paused and stared at the driver. He had a long cut on the side of his face going from his ear to his chin.

Conrad flinched nervously as he stared back at the man. "Ah…Leroy, he grunted. "I don't think I want to go for a ride."

Leroy pushed him into the car and got in.

"You shallow, cold-hearted, manipulative bastard! Get your ass in the fucking car!"

Quickly the limousine driver closed the door after them.

Suddenly the car jerked abruptly and took off.

Conrad adjusted himself and looked on with a frightened expression. He swallowed hard. "Leroy, I don't understand. What's this all about?"

Leroy leaned back in the seat and calmly lit a cigarette. He inhaled deeply. It was obvious he was enjoying watching Conrad squirm.

He took another long drag on his cigarette. He took it out of his mouth and studied it. He fingered the cigarette and blew on the end. It turned a bright red.

In the silence of the moment the seconds ticked by slowly. Conrad sucked in a deep breath.

Leroy maliciously looked up at him and smiled. Quietly he opened the car window and threw out the cigarette. "I can't believe I'm the fucking criminal in this fucking family Conrad!"

Conrad rubbed his jaw and started rocking back and forth. He was scared. "Man, I don't know what you're talking about," he looked mystified. "Besides, you've caught me with a whore before. You said yourself as long as I was discrete…." his voice broke off as he watched the cold eyes that stared back at him. "I haven't done anything. I swear…"

The moment was silent.

Nervously Conrad stared back of Leroy. He could decimate a person just with his bold stare.All at once Conrad knew what he'd just said was as damaging as any confession could ever be.

Leroy leaned over and looked him in the eyes. "You lying ass son of a bitch. Don't you know what conduct befitting a man who claims to love his wife looks like? You don't drug my sister and let some bisexual bitch rape her ass and then think your ass is going to get away with that shit!"

Conrad nervously laughed. His mouth was dry. "Leroy, I don't know what you're talking about, seriously."

"Wham!" Immediately Leroy's hand jerked out and landed another blow. "That's for lying to me a second time!"

On impulse, Conrad's hand released a blow.

Leroy laughed out maliciously. His face contorted viciously, as he punched Conrad's face with fierce precise accuracy. He followed the blows with several well-placed blows to the gut until Conrad grunted unconsciously.

Chapter 35

At last my lover has come...

At the sound of rapid knocking, Pearl rushed to the door. She stopped briefly at the mirror by the door and checked her appearance. She tugged at the ribbon that held her black negligee tight and released it.

Quickly she opened the door wide and took a step back as she watched Louis enter the suite.

"Baby, I'm all yours," Louis said thrusting a bundle of red roses into her arms.

He took in the black negligee and whistled loudly.

Pearl smiled seductively as her eyes gleamed back at him. "Let me guess, you never got a chance to give the winner of the pageant her roses?"

"Nor any of the others," he said nodding. His voice became soft and ameliorating. "Black lace looks good on you by the way."

She buried her face in the blooms and inhaled. "Thank you for the roses and the compliment," she walked gracefully toward the bedroom, swaying her hips as seductively as possible.

"I think there's a vase in here somewhere," she said.

Louis enjoyed the view as she walked past him. He watched her searching for something to hold the flowers. He closed the distance between them and took the flowers from her hand and placed them down on the table in front of them. His eyes flickered over her body like a starving man ready to eat.

"I need to put the flowers in some water," Pearl said, her eyes holding his gaze.

"The flowers can wait, I can't," Louis said in a husky voice, drawing her into his arms.

Pearl felt like weeping. "Louis you've got to make changes next year, The Grand Isle Ball takes up too much of your time."

"I agree with whatever you decide Pearl. I love you," he said kissing her. "I love you, you hear. And I'm not going to let anything ever make you think I don't."

Pearl helped Louis remove his clothes. She pushed the roses off of the table and hopped up on it.

Louis watched her with wild wide-eyed excitement. It only took a moment for him to take her hint.

"The table-top, what an excellent idea Pearl," he hoarsely murmured.

"The table-top for now," she coolly said eyeing him. "But I have plans to make love on every piece of furniture in this suite. Including that bed," she said kissing him.

Louis groaned.

The two lovers were frantic with need from denying themselves for so long. Fingers and hands reached out probing, touching, possessing, like addicts in need of their next fix.

Pearl continued to kiss him with full inviting lips as she let her fingers trickle down his chest until they reached the erogenous zone of the lower part of his body. It immediately got hard.

Shuddering she felt the fire inside her blazing as she touched him.

With a groan Louis' hand slid down and cupped her thighs, spreading them wider.His fingers traced, probing, touching and possessing until he heard her gasp with mindless passionate pleasure as he finally entered her. He rode her with deep primitive animal need, as his lips moved down her shoulders to the nape of her neck before he felt the urgency to again possess her lips.

She surrendered to him completely as he felt his body tighten and explode inside her as they climaxed together.

Chapter 36

Home at last...

The next day, the afternoon sun was shining brightly as Louis drove his white on white Cadillac Deville up Mount Hamilton Road.

The entrance to the private road where their family home sat, off of the mountain, afforded some breathtaking views of the San Jose Valley below them.

Louis drove the car into the driveway and set the parking brake.

"Pearl, are these all the bags?" he asked but didn't wait for a response. "Somehow there seemed to be way less."

"That's because I sent the kids bags with them to Mother Kahina Laveau," she said.

Pearl got out of the car and breathed out a sigh of relief, happy to be home.

"Louis, as soon as I change. How about I fix us a couple of sandwiches for lunch? You'll be hungry after you carry our luggage into the bedroom," Pearl suggested.

"That's a great idea," Louis said nodding and carrying the suitcases into the house.

Pearl followed him to the room and quickly unpacked. She changed into a pair of jeans and a soft light-weight sweater.

An hour later, downstairs in the kitchen, Pearl retrieved the whistling kettle of hot water from the stove and quickly poured it into a black and gold Royal Dutton teapot.

A few minutes earlier she'd quickly made ham and Swiss cheese sandwiches on sourdough bread.

Louis walked into the kitchen, strolled over and kissed Pearl on the cheek.

He loved tranquil happy moments like this. He took a seat at the table.

Pearl arranged a teacup setting in front of him and poured. After which she placed a sandwich in front of him.

He took a bite of his sandwich.

Suddenly the ringing of the telephone startled them.

Pearl and Louis stared between each other.

"Damn, I hope Mother Kahina Laveau hasn't grown tired of the kids already," Louis said breaking the ice.

The telephone rang again.

"I'll get it," Louis said, rising and reaching for the phone.

"Hello", he said.

"Louis this is Ulysses. There's been a terrible accident. I need you to come right away. I'm at Central Valley hospital. We've got a crisis on our hands. There are reporters here asking questions…"

"What…What happened?" Louis demanded, feeling the wind being sucked out of him. He sat down in the chair.

The line went quiet.

"Louis…Louis…Are you still there?" Ulysses wailed into the telephone.

Suddenly Louis felt fear in the pit of his stomach. Something else bad had happened that was connected to the Grand Isle Ball. The event was now starting to leave a bad taste in his mouth. He felt like a man caught in quicksand being pulled under. "Yes, I'm still here. Now what happened?"

Ulysses cleared his throat. "At eleven thirty this morning the maid used her key to open Delilah Deauville's private suite at the top of the hotel. Apparently, she lives there regularly. She owns the suite," he paused. "The maid found her naked and unconscious. And it gets worse. She was straddling a naked man when she was found and he was unconscious too," he gave a snort, pausing, letting the shock of his words sink in. "They had been in the middle of having sex before they both passed out. Damn, I bet their bodies all twisted together was a sight," he joked with a laugh.

"Who was the man?" Louis asked tensely.

"Why it was Monty Wildhorse."

"What?" Louis said as a puzzled expression crossed his face.

"Louis, that is not all. Another naked woman was found in the room with them. She was lying on the chaise. The other woman was Celica Baptiste."

"Celica Baptiste! Are you sure?"

Pearl sucked in a deep breath as instant recognition froze her as she sat. "Celica?" She murmured as her eyes sought out Louis'.

Louis watched a flicker of fear cross Pearl's face as she rose and walked slowly to stand by the kitchen window.

"Okay, Ulysses I'll come right down. You just hold down the fort until I get there. Well, look, I have to go," Louis said ending the call.

Louis hung up the telephone. He turned and walked over and joined Pearl standing by the window. He slipped his arm around her and hugged her.

"Everything is going to be alright Pearl," he said as his voice pulled her back from her memories.

Pearl's eyes brimmed with tears. "Oh Louis, I saw Celica after that fiasco at the queen pageant. She was upset about Monty. I suggested she find another job and stop working for him. She said she didn't have to, like she knew something was about to happen," she said soberly.

"Maybe you're just reading too much into it," he said.

"No, I don't think so. Celica was acting strange. Even crazy like," she suggested and then held his gaze. "And Louis there is more. She was already drunk," she choked out with a worried expression.

"Shhhhh Pearl honey, please don't worry. I'll go down and see what happened."

Chapter 37

A victim of circumstance...

Louis arrived at the hospital within the hour and quickly located Ulysses. The two of them quickly agreed to say whatever was needed to protect the name and reputation of the Foundation and the Grand Isle Ball.

But as fate would have it, they didn't have to really do much. Delilah Deauville's name carried quite a position of power.

The story they concocted and gave the local reporter, that the incident was unconnected to the Grand Isle Ball, seemed believable even to them. And the reporter ate it up quickly and went about his way.

The two old friends watched him leave.

All at once Louis gasped and jerked around as a hand touched his shoulder.

"Hey, Mister!" A man, in faded scrubs, called.

Louis and Ulysses turned around in unison.

A heavy-set man in scrubs approached them.

"Your name is Ulysses, right?" the man asked but didn't wait for a response. "I saw you earlier in Delilah's room."

Ulysses nodded.

"Delilah Deauville said to tell you she wants to see you. And she said to bring Louis with you too."

A few minutes later Louis and Ulysses marched unannounced into Delilah's room.

A commotion inside stopped them abruptly.

"You're a deceitful lying slut Delilah!" an angry Jean Baptiste shouted bitterly. "Celica is your little sister for Christ sake. You should look out for her. Instead, you were screwing the brains out of Monty Wildhorse and letting him give you and your sister drugs."

Delilah felt sick to her stomach as she tried to ignore the angry rage spewing out of Jean Baptiste. He was the only person who she had ever felt any real love from in their family. She hated that he was thinking bad of her. She turned, looked past him and saw the men standing in the doorway.

"Jean, we have visitors," she said gloomily.

Jean stopped his barrage and turned around.

The moment was awkward.

He stared embarrassed. "Louis & Ulysses," he shrugged. "Ignore what I just said. It's a private family matter. I should get going."

Impatient to leave, Jean walked to the door and paused. He turned and looked back thoughtfully at Delilah. "Delilah I'm sorry for yelling. You know how I get. Forgive me," he said meeting her gaze tenderly. "We're still family, no matter how dysfunctional we are. If you need something…"

Even at his most angry and tormented moment Jean's eyes still held a deep level of warmth, care, and love for her.

Delilah's heart quickened as she stared back at him. She softly smiled."Thanks, Jean, I appreciate that."

Jean closed the door behind him.

Before the tears could swell in her eyes Delilah turned her attention to the two men standing in front of her.

"Louis and Ulysses I'm so glad you came," Delilah said with dignity acknowledging their presence.

Both men nodded.

Louis stepped forward and stood at the foot of Delilah's bed. "You know we couldn't resist finding out what happened."

"Guys please have a seat. There's so much I want to say," she said.

Ulysses took a step and scooted in closer as he softly chuckled. "And there is so much we want to hear. Like what really happened between you, Monty and Celica," he softly said. "Oh, and please give as many details as you like," he grinned. "I love a lot of details by the way."

"Please ignore him," Louis shrugged.

Delilah sat quietly for a moment. "I'm a victim of circumstance. I know that this tragic affair happened in my suite, but it wasn't my drugs," she pleaded.

Slowly she filled them in on the details of her rendezvous with Monty. She left out nothing.

Minutes later she looked back at both men. "I told you everything just like I told the detective Manny Rebrand earlier."

Louis swiveled his head around toward her with a shocked expression. "You spoke with Detective Manny Rebrand?"

"Yes," Delilah shook her head. "You know him?"

Louis blinked and nodded yes to her. He then turned his head and silently mouthed something to Ulysses.

Ulysses cleared his throat and said. "Good, he's handling the case?"

Delilah smiled softly. "It looks like you know him well. I hope he's good."

Ulysses shrugged. "Thankfully we do know him. He's pretty helpful. But don't tell him you heard me give him a compliment. I like to keep our relationship on the sort of, we both hate each other, side."

Delilah flashed him a mirthless smile and continued. "Yes, well like I told him. I've done a lot of things in my time. But slipping drugs into people's drinks is not my thing. You see I don't have to. Because I know I'm beautiful," she said wryly. "I know that may sound vain.

But that's the reason why I never need to give anyone drugs to want to sleep with me."

In wide-eyed bewilderment, Louis and Ulysses looked between each other.

Delilah clenched her fist. "Can't you see, someone else fed us the drugs? Please, I need you guys to find out the truth."

"We'll see what we can do Delilah," Louis said clearing his throat signaling Ulysses it was time to leave.

A few minutes later outside in the hallway, Louis said. "From the details Delilah gave us. It sounds like something might have been in the bottles of champagne."

Ulysses stopped abruptly as a frown creased his brow. "I agree with you there. But the lawyer in me wants to know how the drugs got there. If Delilah said she saw Celica open a brand-new bottle of champagne, how did the drugs get into the bottle?"

Central Valley hospital is several huge, tan colored buildings that sit in the heart of Silicon Valley on several acres.

Louis and Ulysses walked off of the elevator to the main floor. They headed for the main entrance.

They walked right smack into Detective Manny Rebrand.

"Hey, Louis and Ulysses. I was told you two were here," Detective Rebrand smiled kindly. His eyes crinkled up when he smiled.

Ulysses' brows lifted in surprised annoyance. "Well, if it isn't detective Manny Rebrand," he said drily.

"Nice to see you again Louis," Detective Manny nodded.

He then glanced at Ulysses. "I heard you are now officially dating Clare Palling."

"Yes, I am. What of it?" Ulysses asked, fixing him with a questioning gaze.

There was an awkward pause.

"Nothing, I just wanted to shake the hand of the man who won over Clare Palling's heart. Let me congratulate you," Manny said extending his hand. "By the way, Clare told me that she is very happy about your dating permanently. And she told me I cannot ask her to dance at next year's ball unless I first check and see if it is okay with you," he said solemnly. "So I guess I'm out of a dance partner at next year's Grand Isle Ball, huh?"

Slowly Ulysses grinned wide, pleased by what he heard. Clare had already let it be known she was his girl. He was happy. "Well, maybe I'll see what I can do for you at next years' ball. Thank you for being happy for me."

Louis smiled and shook his head. "Well now that we've gotten that out of the way, maybe you could help us with this situation Manny. The one that happened after the ball," he said. "From your greeting earlier, I was hoping you had something to tell us."

"Yes, I do. That's why I came to look for you," Manny said. "Did you two know that Delilah and Celica are sisters?"

Louis looked at Ulysses. He shrugged.

"No, she didn't mention it to us," Louis said.

"Well it's a little complicated, Detective Manny said as he decided he'd better hit them with all the details at once. "Delilah was adopted well before Celica was born. In fact, their Mother Pandora was married to her first husband, Anubis Baptiste when the two of them adopted Delilah.

Louis furrowed his brows. "Oh really? Did you notice there is a big difference in Delilah's and Celica's ages?"

Detective Manny nodded. "Yes, there is. There is over ten years between them. But still you know sibling rivalry knows no age," he paused, stuck his hands in his pockets, and continued. "Once her first husband Anubis died, he left Delilah their adopted daughter over half of his property and money. The rest he left to his younger brother, Horus Baptiste. He left Pandora hardly anything," he paused. "Anyway,

Pandora married her first husband's younger brother Horus.Horus already had a son by his first marriage. That son is Jean Baptiste."

"Pandora and Horus," Louis shrugged.

Detective Manny nodded. "The story gets even better if I believe what Delilah told me."

"What?" Louis asked.

"Celica is really Horus Baptiste the younger brother's biological daughter," Detective Manny said. "So that would mean Jean Baptiste and Celica Baptiste are biological brother and sister, same father and same mother."

"Whew!" Ulysses exclaimed. "Louis, did you follow along with all of that story?"

With a puzzled look, Louis shook his head. "About as good as you did Ulysses."

Talk about complicated family relationships. That one is a block-buster," Ulysses said.

Louis cast a sideways glance at Detective Manny. "Was Jean Baptiste living at home when Pandora and Horus married? I mean was he raised with Celica and Delilah?"

"Jean is a few years older than Delilah. As a matter of fact, he was away at college when his father married Pandora. For what I learned, he hardly came home except for holiday visits and the like."

"Hump," Louis said. "What about all that money Delilah inherited. Did she get it right away?"

"No Delilah had to wait until she turned twenty-one. She lived at home until then. They say she made a big production about moving out. Complete with a party at the San Jose Hotel, where she'd bought the top floor suite and made it resemble an ancient Roman house. She's lived there ever since."

"Hmm," Louis said thoughtfully.

Detective Manny stared between the two men and continued. "I learned that Horus and Pandora Baptiste were in a car accident five years after Delilah moved out. Horus died at the scene, but Pandora died at this hospital. Celica was with her when she died. Their son Jean Baptiste was married to Pauline by then. He and Pauline took Celica in and raised her, along with a woman called Aunt Dolly Baptiste. She is Pandora's sister."

Ulysses' eyes clouded over with disappointment. "So that's about it? It sounds like normal family stuff."

"Well, I haven't finished. I learned that Celica hates Delilah because she's been in love with Monty Wildhorse several years. And no matter what she did. Monty wouldn't give her the time of day. He didn't love her back. Anyway, to make a long story short, Celica put the drug in the Champagne. We found a kit in her home complete with bottles of Monty Wildhorse's private label unopened champagne bottles. Celica owned some corking equipment."

"Expensive equipment," Ulysses said shaking his head. "I'm a wine connoisseur."

"Really?" Louis blurted out with a deep expression of shock. "I always thought you were a straight bourbon man."

Ulysses shrugged. "Very funny."

Detective Rebrand scratched his head. "You know the most amazing part. I wouldn't have figured it out. I mean thinking that Celica had done it. I had never suspected her. I had suspected Delilah of putting the drugs in the champagne."

"What made you change your mind? About considering Celica as your suspect," Louis asked with a puzzled expression.

Detective Manny took a deep breath. "Celica called me and asked me to come to her room. She told me she wanted to tell me something. When I got there, she kept staring at the wall like someone was standing there," the color drained from his face.

Suddenly there was a relative silence as Louis and Ulysses stared back at him.

Detective Manny's face looked stricken and there was a level of fear in his voice. "The next thing I knew, Celica started talking to thin air. I thought it was the drugs she had taken," his eyes glassed over dazed.

"But then a cold air brushed past me and I felt like I was looking at the room through a fog."

Louis and Ulysses cast glances between them. The moment was awkward.

All at once Detective Manny jabbed his hands in his pockets shaking his head as if to clear his thoughts as he continued. "I'm not one for going in for believing all of that Louisiana hocus pocus stuff. But there was something strange happening in Celica's room," he said staring off into space. "I don't know, but it was really strange and creepy, the way Celica kept staring at the wall. She kept saying she had a change of heart and that she couldn't go on hating Delilah because Delilah had been a motherless girl who had to do what people around her made her do. She said Delilah was her sister and that love was stronger than hate. She then told me it had been her plan to make it look like Delilah had drugged their drinks."

"What?" Louis and Ulysses said in unison.

Detective Manny turned and gave Louis and Ulysses a serious look. He let out a sigh of frustration. "I've been puzzling over whether or not I should tell anyone this. For the record fellas, this one is off the record. You see I did ask Celica what she was looking at and she told me it was a lady. Then she described to me what the lady looked like. She said she was wearing a white tee shirt and white jeans and that she had a mass of curly jet-black hair and deep luminous blue eyes. She said the eyes were what made her tell me the truth that she'd done it. She said the woman's eyes looked just like Delilah's," he murmured, his voice held a mysterious tone as he continued. "You see, for a minute I thought I might have been hallucinating or something, because all of a sudden I saw the woman Celica said was in the room with her. She didn't look like a hallucination at all. In fact, she looked like an angel, an angel who looked exactly like Delilah."

The moment was eerie and silent.

Louis broke the silence. "Hump, that was creepy," he shrugged feeling a shiver.

"Yeah, too creepy," Ulysses muttered under his breath.

173

Chapter 38

❧

A Wish...

Days later Delilah Deauville sat in her hospital room waiting. She felt like a caged animal alone and frightened. For the first time, she realized how alone she was in the world. She rarely felt low times like this. She'd always kept herself busy. Because low times like this made her think of her mother, she felt a deep emptiness inside. It made her shiver.

Her half-brother Jean Baptiste had promised to come and sign her out and take her home. But he hadn't returned yet from getting Celica squared away at a treatment facility.

Jean Baptiste had instructed the hospital not to release her until he returned.

Delilah sighed and walked over to the window. "God, I wish I had someone who loved me," she murmured low against the window.

A moment later.

"Good morning are you ready to go?" A familiar voice called out to her.

"It's you!" she blurted standing paralyzed in the spot where she stood.

The man closed the door behind himself as he walked closer into the room. He looked handsome, rugged and notorious. His wavy black hair was pulled back in a ponytail.

Slowly he reached into his jacket pocket and pulled out an eye glass case. He put on a pair of black-rimmed glasses.

"Damn, Leroy Maddox Jefferson, you always look like a loveable Geek-King whenever you put on those glasses," she said shaking her head. What do you want?"

A smile tugged at the corners of his mouth as he closed the distance between them. "First, I want to make sure I see you clearly," he said. "Then I would assume it is obvious I've come to claim the girl that I love and take you home. Preferably to my place and not that Roman style tower mess you call a home."

Delilah felt her senses reeling. She turned and looked at him. His eyes were filled with pain. "How could you still love me, Maddy? Knowing what I am, what I..." she said her voice trailing off laced with deep sadness. "Not after all the things I've done to you?"

He made a soft sound as her words caught him off guard. "What about me? What about the embarrassing stupid stuff I've done over the years that ended up being in the news? I'm the most notorious Geek-King Street-thug in Oakland. Some say, in all of northern California. But you never cared about what people said about me. It never stopped you from loving me."

"Oh, Maddy don't you see. Every time you look at me you'll hate me for what I've done. You don't know what it is I've done this time," she tried to tell him but the words wouldn't leave her tongue.

"Oh Delilah," a primitive groan came out of his throat as he said her name. "In all the years we've known each other haven't I demonstrated that I love, respect, accept, cherish and desire you?"

"But this time is different," she said. Her thoughts raced. How could she tell him what it was she had done? She stood there stunned, thinking about it.

He nervously walked over to the window and stared out. "I meant what I said Delilah, I don't care. I've got way more important issues to deal with in this world than what it is you think you've done that's so bad."

Delilah watched him tormented and frustrated. He was the only man she had ever loved. His unselfish admiration, love, and kindness toward her were the one constant she could ever count on. He was the only man she had ever trusted. The only man she had ever loved. Even now her love for him was going stronger because she knew he carried their secret. No one else in the world knew about their secret but her and her Maddy.

From somewhere deep inside she had to say it. She put her hands over her face. "Oh Maddy, you know I'm sorry for what I've done. I do have some morals and values. Conrad slipped something into my drink just like Celica did. I'm not making excuses for my behavior. I should have known better. I don't know why. I just have to say that to you. You forgive me don't you?"

He closed the distance between them in one stride and took her in his arms. He held her close and said. "I knew you would tell me the truth and you know I've forgiven you. Besides, since we're being honest, I want you to know I kicked Conrad's ass for what he did. I kicked his ass really good."

Delilah softly laughed. "I bet you did," she said. "And I just wish I'd been there to see you tear into him. We are so much alike. That's what I love about you, Maddy. You're always looking out for me," she softly smiled.

She looked at the distress in his face. After a long pause, she said. "Are you okay?"

"I'm okay. Look, Delilah, I have a proposition for you. I want us to get married. I'm playing all my cards out on the table. I love you and I want to grow old with you," his voice trailed off. He cleared his throat and rattled on like a drowning man trying to save himself by whatever means necessary. "I'm tired of raising our little girl alone. She needs a mother," Leroy's lips quivered. "And if you are not ready to change, I'm going to sign over rights to our little girl to my sister Ming and let her raise her."

She stared at him dazed. "What?"

"You heard me."

"Maddy, you'd use blackmail on me?"

His lips tightened. He instinctively knew he had played all his cards. There was no turning back. "Yes!" he assuredly said.

"And you are insisting that I marry you?" she asked.

"Yes!" he yelled.

The moment was tense.

"Leroy Maddox Jefferson, I was going to say yes when you said you loved me. You didn't have to lay all your cards out on the table. I know it has been hard for you raising our daughter. But you know I'm going to say yes because I don't want Ming or anybody else raising my daughter, but me."

He drew her close to him as his lips kissed hers.

"Promise me Maddy you'll always be there for me and our daughter."

"I promise", he whispered softly kissing her.

Dear Gentle Readers...

Dear Gentle Readers, Fans, Family and Friends,
Reviews for my books are what this author needs... Let me explain.

In an effort to provide you with the most honest information about me. I confess I am a self-published author.

That's right, I am committed to writing a story, a novel every chance I get (hopefully I will put out two to three books a year). Even though I have a whacked-out, frenetic, hectic schedule as do many others. I persevere. I am committed to writing my stories.

With that said, I'd like to make a request of you my gentle readers, followers, friends, and family. I appreciate that you read my books. And I need you to please go to Amazon.com or KINDLE and review my book.

I will be truthful if you do. I would like for you to help me.

Your kindness to me in reviewing my books would go a long way in helping me continue my self-publishing journey.

Thank you for all that you do. I truly appreciate you!
Sincerely,

J. A. Jackson
Email: jerreecejackson@gmail.com

179

Books by J. A. Jackson

A Geek an Angel Series

The Grand Hotel
Lovers, Players, & The Seducer
Lovers, Players, Revenge

XXX

The Mistress of Desire
& The Orchid Lover
Book I & Book II

XXX
The Deceiver Secret Book I

XXX

Stand Alone Books
The Deceiver
The Proposition

Books by J. A. Jackson

When A Taker Dreams

Diamond at Midnight

Thank You Readers & Fans!

To All My Fans & Readers…

Thank you for all that you do! I'm humbled and grateful.

Thank you!

J. A. Jackson

About the Author

J. A. JACKSON is an author who lives in an enchanted little house she calls home in the Northern California foothills with her husband and Big Sally an American scent hound. She fell in love with writing as a small child. She was born in Arkansas and comes from a family rich in story tellers. She spent over ten years working in the non-profit sector where she wrote grants, press releases and contributed many stories to their newsletter. She was their Newsletter editor for over ten years. She loves growing roses, a good pot of hot tea, chocolate, magical stories, suspense stories, ghost stories, and reading Jane Austen again and again in her pastime. Please write her at P.O. Box 612751 San Jose, CA 95161.

This Novel was written by Jerreece Ann Jackson
Pseudonym: J. A. Jackson
P.O. Box 612751
San Jose, CA 95161

MEDIA CONTACT: Jerreece Jackson
Email: **jerreecejackson@gmail.com**

You can connect with me on:
🌐 http://jerreeceannjackson.blogspot.com
🐦 https://twitter.com/jerreece
f https://www.facebook.com/JerreeceJackson/?ref=bookmarks
🔗 https://www.goodreads.com/author/show/7515379.J_A_Jackson/blog

Subscribe to my newsletter:
✉ https://mailchi.mp/ddf9555be2a4/theauthorjajackson

Also by J. A. Jackson

Prepare to lose yourself in a fascinating world of romance, intrigue and sultry secrets, a world of decadence, adventure and excitement, a world you'll never want to leave!

The Deceiver's Secret!
Enter the world of Eve Lafoy- a world filled with decadent parties, sultry encounters, and a fabulous nightlife. A world inhabited by jealousy and betrayal.

Lovers, Players & The Seducer Book I

Lust and passion fueled star-crossed lovers Lacey & Kienan. Their love was packed with angst and heartbreak from the start. And her brother Nicholas is addicted to deceitful games. When tragic forces are unleashed family lines are crossed revealing secret sins and shameful lies from the past. A past where the dead watch the living. A vengeful seducer is unleashed. Life will never be the same in this gripping shocking twist-filled story of love, lies, and redemption!

www.ingramcontent.com/pod-product-compliance
Lightning Source LLC
Chambersburg PA
CBHW050531190726
48284CB00003B/1028